RITES OF
AUTUMN

Cliff Schimmels

VICTOR
BOOKS a division of SP Publications, Inc.
WHEATON. ILLINOIS 60187

Offices also in
Whitby, Ontario, Canada
Amersham-on-the-Hill, Bucks, England

Library of Congress Catalog Card Number: 85-50325
ISBN: 0-89693-334-2

VICTOR BOOKS
A division of SP Publications, Inc.
        Wheaton, Illinois 60187

Contents

CLIFF SCHIMMELS calls on his rural background in Oklahoma and his love for football to examine the father-son relationship in *Rites of Autumn*. He taught English and coached football in a town similar to Wheatheart before coming to Wheaton College in 1974 as Professor of Education.

Dr. Schimmels is the author of four books on education and the home, including *How to Help Your Child Survive and Thrive in the Public Schools* (Revell). Cliff and his wife, Mary, have three children.

———————————

The smells and sounds of rural Oklahoma,
a sunset lingering in the West,
a cow grazing on the distant hill,
freshly plowed dirt, diesel smoke,
the growth and harvest of wheat—
it was all a part of my growing.
It is an inseparable part of me still.

To those people who taught me such things
as honesty, sincerity, loyalty, and the honor of work,
to those who opened their lives and invited me in,
I offer these Chronicles as a token of my gratitude.
I love you and cherish our times together
both in the present and in my remembering.

Cliff Schimmels
1985

Good night, sweet prince
And flights of angels sing thee to thy rest!

———————

SHAKESPEARE
Hamlet V, ii

1

The Dust of Fallen Dreams
1981

"Abe! Oh, Abe! Yoo-hoo, Abe Ericson! Wait a minute, Abe!"

Trapped! Right in the middle of Main Street—halfway between the safety of his pickup truck and the front door of the Culligan Soft Water place. Old Mrs. Strommer, the champion gossip in town, was bearing down on him. She wasn't cruel. She just talked too much, and right then he wasn't in the mood to talk to anyone, or to be talked to directly. But like a chicken in the middle of a dusty road with a wheat truck rumbling by, Abe couldn't go forward and he couldn't go back; so he just humped up and waited for the onslaught.

"Abe, I want you to know that I am, well, the whole town, is just sick about what happened. Just sick to death."

"Yes, ma'am.' He had already heard this, somewhere between a thousand and a million times, so he had learned just what to say, or at least what people expected him to say. Did he ever dare say what he wanted to? Probably not. She was just being kind. Besides she talked so much he didn't have time to think about what he wanted to say.

"Jimmy Charles was always such a sweet boy, Abe. Everybody

just thought so much of him." And with this, tears began to build in her eyes. She turned her head to one side and sobbed with a subdued rhythm.

At this, Abe reached out to her—not physically, he wasn't that kind of person. But he reached out to her with his feelings in such a way that she could sense it. He just stood there and watched quietly, but he was sure that she felt his support. And Abe was bitterly amused with the turn of events. She was supposed to be comforting him, and here he was, giving her solace. He wanted to cry himself. He wanted to cry until every gutter in town overflowed with his tears and the people had to walk through the mud. That's what he wanted to do. He did not want to stand there comforting his comforter. But it was what he should do, so he did it. He was a man. He was strong. And strong men help women when they cry.

With his emotional support to lean on, she dried her sobs and got right back in the conversation, just as he knew she would.

"How's Mary Ruth taking it, Abe?"

"Fine. She's just fine, Mrs. Strommer."

That was a lie. Abe didn't know how Mary Ruth was, but he knew she wasn't fine. How could anyone ever really know how anyone else ever is? Hers was a dumb question, asking someone to report on someone else's feelings. Abe couldn't climb inside Mary Ruth's head and heart and measure the hurt. But he knew it was there, just as he knew his hurt was there, even if he couldn't describe it.

During the events of the past week, Abe had realized that he didn't know all that much about the feelings that came with being a father. He knew even less about what mothers feel at times like these. All he could do was to go by Mary Ruth's actions. She got up every morning just as she always had. She fixed breakfast, and tidied up a house which hadn't been lived in since the last time she tidied it the morning before. She talked to Abe about the chores and about what people had said and about the price of wheat and the need for rain, and about what duties they had to do through the next few days.

If this was fine, then she was fine. But Abe knew that underneath there was more, and that the part underneath wasn't fine. Mary Ruth didn't give any clues, none that you could see; but Abe knew there was something there as turbulent as an April hail cloud. He knew it was there, and that someday he and Mary Ruth would have to face it. He didn't understand why they had to face it, not really. In fact, he wondered if other people around Wheatheart would face that storm if they were in the same situation. He doubted if they would, and that made him wonder if it would be a show of weakness in him to stand by and let his own wife express her feelings honestly and completely, regardless of who got in the way.

"Well," Mrs. Strommer went on with civic immunity to what Abe was feeling and thinking, "I still say it was a wasteful tragedy. That's what it was. Just tragic. Such a fine boy. And gone to waste like that. But Abe," and he could tell that she was going to change directions, "didn't you think Brother Bob's sermon was nice? Yes, it was. It was so nice. I have heard lots of people say how nice it was. Nice sermons at times like these mean so much to the living. They really do. Well, I remember the sermon he preached at my husband's. . . ."

Words. Words. Abe interrupted her chatter with his own thoughts. Brother Bob's sermon was only words. How could words be nice? And even if they were, how could people know what was happening to him? How could Brother Bob understand? What did he know about death? What did he know about sons and about football? How could any of them—Brother Bob, old Mrs. Strommer, or even Mary Ruth? They couldn't know that the biggest pain of all was that the dreams had stopped. Like young wheat plants starved for moisture, the dreams had withered and mingled into the red dust. Words weren't nice, not even the right ones. They were only dusty words.

"Well, Abe," Mrs. Strommer was winding down, probably tiring from her little game of making him feel better. "I must run on. I just wanted you to know how much we all care. Let us know if we can help. You know me. I'm always home when you need me."

"Yes, ma'am. Thank you, ma'am."

"And I guess you'd better get on about your business. You probably have a lot of things to tend to." She was noticeably stronger now that she had unloaded her sympathy.

"Yes, ma'am. I was just going in to send a telegram."

"Oh, yes. Well, I think I heard someone say you can do that right there in the water store. Don't know for sure. Never sent one myself. But I guess you can find out. Well. Bye, Abe."

"Good-bye, ma'am." And Abe rushed on into the Culligan Soft Water place before he was caught in the dry dust again.

"Hi, Ed."

"Hello, Abe." Ed Rogers barely looked up from his intensive endeavor at repairing the ancient cash register that sat in the middle of the dividing counter.

"You know, Ed, I don't recall ever being in this building before." This was a painful admission for Abe, because he thought he had been in every building on Main Street at some time; but just in case, he inventoried the high ceiling, the worn marbled floors, the naked cord which had once suspended the massive four-bladed fan, and assorted water-softener equipment stacked in a rather orderly display about the room.

"Think not?" Even for small talk, Ed Rogers was an enigma. In his khaki pants and print shirt, he was a clean-hands tinkerer who through a variety of jobs about town had always managed to make a living for himself, his wife, and his three band-playing daughters, without getting next to the soil. Abe had known Ed since high school, but never well. Ed had quit the football team his senior year to take a correspondence course in some kind of higher math, and as far as Abe knew, had never had close friends since. Although he had lived in Wheatheart all his life, Ed Rogers seemed like a transient.

"You have been here with the Culligan business four or five years, haven't you?" Abe made it sound like a "long time, no see" friendly gesture.

"It will be eleven years in February."

This didn't sting, nor was it meant to. Time lapse is not a scientific item in small towns.

"Do you also handle the telegraph business?" Abe asked, despite the small Western Union sign in the window. Elapsed time also outdates store signs.

"Yep, ever since the depot closed."

"Well, I had heard that. I want to send a telegram."

Ed was still casual, "I have kind of been expecting you."

Abe remembered why he had always hated Ed Rogers. His blunt perception always took the mystery and romance out of the unexpected and noble.

"You'll have to help me. I am sorta new at it. This is the first time in my life I ever sent a telegram." His voice and reflection trailed off. "I've done a lot of things this week I never did before." The concept of the week startled him. Had it been just a week, all of a week, or had it been years and years? How could all that emotion be wrapped up in just one week?

"I know what you mean. I went through the same thing a few years ago when I lost my folks." This was as close to sympathy as Abe was going to get. "Here's a pad. Write down what you want to say."

Abe took the pad and the First State Bank pen, and then hesitated. "Well, Mary Ruth and I talked this out this morning, but now I don't know how to say it. I want it to be just right." If Ed read the frustration, he gave no indication nor assistance.

"Okay." Abe grabbed some confidence from the stillness. "What do you think of this? 'To Coach Rose and the Whippets: Best wishes for a victory tonight. That's the way Jimmy Charles would have wanted it. I am sure he is with you in spirit. Signed, Abe and Mary Ruth Ericson' "

"That's a lot more words than the ten you're allowed." Ed was practical.

"Can't I pay extra and say all that?"

"Sure, that comes to $3.55 plus an extra dime for the governor."

"There's tax on everything these days," Abe complained customarily, as he handed Ed four one-dollar bills.

Ed made change from the semirepaired cash register and offered a semigenuine, "Thanks."

"Oh," Abe remembered. "When will this be delivered?" Timing was important with some messages.

"I'll send it down there this afternoon and ask them to deliver it to the dressing room at about 7:30." For a guy who didn't show much interest, Ed knew a lot about football. Or was he making fun of all of it?

Abe decided not to push the matter any further. "See ya." And he walked to the door.

As he stepped off the stoop of the Culligan Soft Water place and into the November sunlight that Friday morning, Abe made two decisions. The first was immediate, and decisive. He decided to have his midmorning coffee and conversation at the Dew Drop Inn Cafe instead of at the John Deere Store. But that decision was based on a brief but thorough survey of Main Street.

For all practical purposes, Main Street began at the John Deere store where two Quonset perpendicular business barns rose out above the green and gold machinery scattered about with hurried purpose. To the north, business houses and vacant storefronts lined both sides for two long blocks. Up and down the street, the permanent and the transient stood side by side. There were the old landmarks: the variety store; Jones Grocery—although no one knew how the old man stayed in business anymore; the two commercial banks facing each other on the south corners of the state highway— Wheatheart might be small, but it was prosperous; Schmidt Hardware; the drugstore, and upstairs, the doctor's office; the old picture show marquee, a reminder of an age long since past; and the Dew Drop Inn Cafe. The cafe was itself a part of the permanent; it had always been there, but with transient management and transient names. The local folks, weary of the lack of tradition, had labeled it a few years ago; and since Dew Drop was quick and easy, the name became as permanent as the building.

For Abe, these were more than landmarks. They were the sights and sounds, the smells and images, of life itself. These were memories and reminders, the present and the future. These were where he went when he went to town, and going to town still brought boyish thrills, even though he was forty years old.

Transients and vacants filled the gaps on the street: a pool hall, insurance agencies, a gift store run by some people who moved in from California, a law office, the Pentecostal Church.

Past the two-block business district were the old firehouse, used mostly for midwinter domino games; the new Methodist Church; the Baptist Church; and several larger, older homes. And, finally, up the hill was the high school, the sentinel of the north with the flagpole flying the colors of America and Oklahoma in the exact center of Main Street. The water tower, standing tall in the west recorded the climbing courage and painting skills of past senior classes. Some classes had taken pride in heights, some in cliches, and some in calligraphy.

Eight towering poles framed the back of the high school. There was no citizen in Wheatheart who did not comprehend and appreciate the symbolic significance of those eight poles and the two rows of floodlights that capped each one. Used no more than seven or eight times each fall, these lights illuminated the battleground of village prestige. Here was the football field, Wheatheart's year-round diversion, yet, more than diversion, its hope and memory.

From the John Deere store on up to the high school, Abe saw it all. He saw it as a prairie farmer sees the pasture when he counts his cows. For Abe, it was all background. As background, it didn't register in his consciousness because there was nothing amiss. If something had been out of place, an unusual automobile, a puff of smoke, a school child on the street, then Abe would have recorded it, for he felt a son of his background. That's what it meant to be a native—this ability to relate to the uniqueness of the background. And the natives like Abe knew this to be the difference between small towns and cities.

Big cities are distinct in their specifics. Abe had seen the Sears Tower, the Alamo, the St. Louis Arch, the Plaza, and the Texas Stadium, and each one of those wonders stood distinct in his mind; but those wonders, those landmarks, those specifics became the symbols of their cities. Small towns, on the other hand, are distinct in their backgrounds. As a native, Abe knew this, and he had short tolerance for people who dismissed Wheatheart as just another small town in the short-grass section of the Southwest. It was *not* just another town; it was Wheatheart, distinctively Wheatheart. John Deere places may all look alike to visitors and transients, but three generations of possessive rugged individualism had left marks on the Wheatheart John Deere store that only a native could see. Wheatheart was the chemistry of all its generations and all its stores and all its permanent and transient residents.

This Friday in November of 1981, the chemistry was in tune. Only Moss Bosco was unusual, with his white beard and hair blowing out from the French beret, and he wasn't really out of place. Moss had been busy all week, hand-lettering signs on the store windows; this Friday morning, he was just adding the aesthetics to his masterpiece on the plate glass windows on the south side of the drugstore. Although his art work was still satisfactory, by this time Moss had used up all the clever slogans, so this sign, in its typical green and white, said simply, "Win with Whippets." Put into the context of all the other green and white windows, the sign read like the last chapter of a book of congratulations and best wishes to the Whippet football team, already district champions and hoping for more. This was Moss's community service project, his livelihood and his bridge to the town, over the chasm of his idiosyncrasies. Throughout the week, Abe and the other natives had measured his progress day by day, as he eradicated the store window memories of the red, white, and blue Fourth of July Rodeo and had brought the town into a green and white season of autumn and football.

With nothing out of place, Abe's choice of coffee at the Dew

Drop over the John Deere store was based on the narrow reality of pickup trucks. His comparative analysis went beyond ownership, although he knew to whom each truck belonged. Identifying machines was a part of the regional virility rites. Early in life Abe had learned to recognize from a half-mile distance every tractor, combine, and plow in the area. Pickups were particularly distinguishable. Although they still carried the characteristics of mass production, each had long since been tooled special by the village blacksmith and had become an instrument of identification and description. From the front bumper hitch to the location of the CB antenna to the gun rack to the tool box to the endgate to the bumper stickers which read, "Crime doesn't pay, but neither does farming!," "Pass with caution: Driver chewing tobacco!" or "Goat ropers need love too!" each machine was a personal paragraph. From early morning when the farmer first drove his vehicle from the house to the barn to begin the day's activities, his pickup served as his castle, his mobility, his alter ego; and he was never far away from it.

But Abe's decision about the Dew Drop Inn was based on more than truck ownership. He saw beyond who had driven those pickups into the parking stalls and vacated them for coffee and fellowship. From their appearance on the streets, Abe could decide the nature of the conversation within. By the way the machines rested, he could tell whether the drivers were in a hurry. By the telltale equipment marks, he could tell what was foremost on the minds of the farmer-owners.

The pickups in front of the John Deere store all indicated haste and farm problems. These men were in town only momentarily. They had work to do, so the conversation would be brief and concerned chiefly with wheat prices and the possibility of rain. The pickups at the Dew Drop indicated leisure. These farmers had already completed morning chores and were in town for as long as the talk was satisfying. Abe particularly noticed the dirt. In front of the John Deere store, the machines were covered with the red dust of plowed fields, representative of the serious business of farming, of getting the maize stubble plowed or the wheat sowed before the next shower. The machines at the Dew Drop were just as dirty, but with grayer matter, caked on by days of wind and rain itself, dirt picked up along the edges of cattle feed lots, representative of the semiserious business of farming, of feeding a few steers out to pad the income a bit this year, with wheat prices so unstable.

Although he had some maize stubble he could be plowing himself, Abe opted for the leisure pace of the Dew Drop. The events and conversation at the Culligan Soft Water store had choked him, and he needed to wash his mind clear with thinner brew.

Abe Ericson made two decisions from that stoop on that Friday morning in mid-November. The first was quick, decisive, as he started toward his coffee. The second decision had taken longer to make, perhaps as long as his lifetime, or perhaps as long as eternity itself. It was the decision of one man alone, the closing scene of a common tale told through this man's hurts and memories played out against the town that set rules for his life and his values.

A Standard of Comparison
1965

March 24, 1965 was a day that demanded to be remembered. For the Oklahoma wheat farmers, it became distinguished as a day that housed one of those severe freaks of nature, one of the worst dust storms of the sixties. There were lesser dust storms during that stormy decade, but this day became the standard of comparison. For years after, the conversation at the John Deere store accepted this distinction. As the farmers complained of the present drought, they would frequently conclude with the ominous warning, directed at no one in particular, "If we don't get some rain soon, we are going to be just right to get something like we had back in March of '65."

Ironically, this was the day Abe Ericson became a father, and that event overshadowed the dust for him. Afterward, when the John Deere discussion turned to storm recollections, Abe bowed out of the one-up-manship games being played with the stories and took a few minutes to look into his own subconscious reality.

Abe got up early that morning of March 24, with a sense of urgency usually reserved only for harvesttime, and occasionally for planting time when the rains come unpredictably. The weatherman on the ten o'clock news the night before had diagrammed the conditions on his map. By 1965, those big weather maps on the ten o'clock news had become a way of life for wheat farmers. Although they had not really changed the actual applied behavior of farming, partly because farmers have few options and also because they seek few, those graphic illustrations of modern-day prophecies of the changing moods of God had at least made the farmers more nervous in their traditional tasks. Abe was particularly nervous this day. The maps had shown a stationary low pressure area near the Arkansas border and a rising high pressure system moving in from Colorado, with no rain in sight. This meant only one thing—wind; and wind meant dirt. Since planting time in the fall, there had not been enough rain or snow to wet the ground and provide the young wheat plants the moisture nourishment needed to entice their roots deep into the earth so that the tops could bush out plentifully and cover the red dirt with the green of life and promise. This spring there were too many open spaces and not enough plants. The exposed soil, caked by recent teasing showers, would fly away into the fence rows, the wind breaks, the pasture lines, and beyond. Like a plantation owner fighting Sherman, like a homesteader fighting a raiding horde of opportunist sooners of the land rush days, Abe had to defend his land.

Although he awoke early, morning was already a gritty sunlight as he hastened through his ritual chores—feeding a few chickens, watering the horse and the feed lot steer kept for butchering purposes, and making talk with Mary Ruth over the breakfast ham and eggs about such matters as the price of chicken feed, the supply of home-cured ham, and the next trip to town. Throughout this conversation, he watched for hints of any change in the way she felt or for indications of apprehension she might be harboring. Of course, the doctor had said that it was still two weeks away, but these things are always so indefinite. His was only a guess, and there was cause for apprehension. Thus, Abe studied the conversation closely hunting for any hints, but he did not ask outright. It never occurred to him to ask.

Abe had an urge to stay close enough to Mary Ruth for her to know that he was concerned. But that was a strange urge which didn't really fit; so instead, he surrendered to the more manly urge of saving his soil. Thus, he hurried to the shed where his equipment was. It was not by accident that his pickup, his tractor, and his rotary hoe (a light implement fixed with a multitude of revolving fingers which pricked into the dirt just below the surface and brought whatever moisture there might be to the top to stabilize the soil) were in the barn; and Abe realized this as he hooked the machinery together. Men who were transients in the farming business would have to search the fields and the dust this morning for their equipment which had been left indiscriminately where it had last been used; but Abe was a permanent and his was in the barn.

With his pickup in tow, Abe's equipment might have reminded a visitor of a circus train, as he made his way to the old Cole place. In this area, each farm bears a special name, usually that of its homesteader. All the land was distributed to homesteaders in 1896, 160 acres to each; but in such a rugged activity as farming, the more rugged soon enlarged their holdings at the expense of the less rugged. Although the Cole place had been in the Ericson family for more than seventy years, it still bore the name of its original owner. It also had its own personality, and one of its emotional quirks was that it was subject to wind.

On this day of universal grit, Abe was not surprised to discover that the situation was even worse here. The dirt in the air formed a red buttress which protected the farm from a roadside view. The fence rows of barbed wire fortified with thistles were presently keeping the high-flying real estate within the boundaries, but this would change soon unless something was done. Abe unhooked the pickup in an out-of-the-way corner and went to work.

With long passages, he cut the field diagonally, working across the currents of the wind. As the curved fingers of the rotary hoe pricked through the crust of the soil, damper, deeper, redder dirt was lifted to the surface. This freshly liberated loam lay still at the top and pulled the blowing sand to it. Abe was achieving his purpose; he was winning the battle; he was bringing order to chaos; he was saving his land. With these feelings of accomplishment, the morning hours went quickly for him.

For some farmers, driving a tractor is a lonely occupation. The high seat does afford a panoramic view of the prairie, plowed and planted, pliable to the whims of the farmer and weather; but those who can not see details soon tire of the prairie, thinking that it all looks alike. They miss the whirlwinds and dust patterns, the shadows at noon, trees standing alone or in bunches, hawks overhead looking for rabbits in the undergrowth, a mother cow standing upwind of her nursing calf, spots of clay rising out of the sand probably marking the buffalo wallows of an age long past.

The wide spaces of western Oklahoma also provide an insightful tractor driver the isolation necessary to become aware of his own existence. Since the present is rarely eventful enough to demand attention, and since there are no other people in view, time is suspended. The successful driver is one who is not afraid to accept the fact of his being. He has the ability to manipulate time, past and future, a future built on past and aspiration, a past interpreted through future and aspiration. Abe was not just a successful tractor driver—he was passionate about it; and this morning was pleasantly filled with haunting pasts and promising futures.

Like the business executive who feels good about "covering a lot of ground" during a particular session, Abe felt a sense of accomplishment. He enjoyed watching the rotary hoe massage his land and bring it to lively patterns of color and texture created by the swirling dirt, and he liked being Abe, past and future.

There were times to remember, and Abe liked to remember. He remembered the Cherokee game during his junior year of high school. The Whippets were behind 14—8 late in the fourth quarter, when he recovered a fumble from his defensive end position. The events were so firmly imprinted on Abe's remembering machinery that they were not really images but real life being relived each time they came to mind. He felt the quarterback slip out from behind the center and sprint down the line of scrimmage toward him. Abe read the option immediately, and he knew what he had to do. Abe always knew what he had to do. That's what Coach Rose had said at the football banquet his senior year. In fact, those were his exact words, "This young man, Abe Ericson, is coachable. In the four years he has played, he has always known what he was supposed to do." And when the option came toward him, he was to hit the quarterback. That's what he did. He moved toward the ball carrier, lowered his head and drove it straight into the back's chest. That's the way Coach Rose had taught him to tackle, head into the numbers. Seeing him coming, the quarterback started to pitch, but Abe's blow was too vicious and the ball rolled onto the grass. What a sight! The brown football bobbing through the green blades of the bermuda grass was a fish on the wharf, an orphan in a custody fight. Abe dived toward it, right at the feet of the trailing back; he curled in a fetal position and warded off grabbing hands and shoulders with his knees. After eons of struggling and fighting, the referee's whistle blew. Abe felt the release of pressure as bodies were being lifted from him; and as soon as he dared, he looked at his arms curled beneath his body and discovered that the wandering child belonged to him. Although dazed with ecstasy, he heard the crowd, felt the accepting pats of his teammates, and heard Assistant Coach Rambo yell encouragement. That was not just another significant event. It was part of all the nuances and all the traits and all the feelings and all the values that added together to make Abe Ericson a person.

Through a sequence of events, directed partly by chance, Abe would now become a local hero. Grade school children would imitate him in their football games. People at the drug store and the John Deere store would congratulate him. Mr. Casteel, the superintendent, would stop him in the hall just to chat. In fact, in this area where farmers operate on credit, bankers have been known to lend money on less collateral than that. From this moment forward, Abe Ericson would be one of Wheatheart's distinguished and trustworthy citizens. . . .

However, on the very next play, Scott Garland of the John Deere Garlands, threw a forty-three-yard touchdown pass to his younger brother, Chuck. On the following Tuesday, Scott was named the player of the week in the *Wheatheart Journal*.

From vivid memories to hazes, Abe's mind brushed the dust from four years of experiences, four Oklahoma football seasons, enough to last a man a lifetime if he worked at it occasionally, and Abe worked at it—isolated plays in isolated games, specific moves and moods and images and feelings during the practices and the games were intensified and interpreted through years of reliving. Abe was a native of Wheatheart, and high school football was part of his reality.

This morning, Abe's mind flowed as free as the tumbleweeds which were riding the winds to the fence rows. Thoughts of farming, neighbors, the John Deere Garlands, his father, his grandfather, and Mary Ruth whistled and mingled through the football storage.

He and Mary Ruth had known each other since childhood. Her folks farmed over by the river, and although river bottom farming was different from farming on the flats, Abe and Mary Ruth had formed a common bond through the Baptist Church in town. It was a factor of community convenience for them to date during high school, and their marriage was just as convenient. The local people knew all the parties involved, so there was no need to adjust to strangers. For the most part, Abe and Mary Ruth's life together was as convenient as its initiation.

They loved each other. At least as far as Abe could tell, they did. But he wasn't sure he knew exactly what love was or how to feel it or even express it. Mary Ruth defined it for him sometimes, but that didn't help much. The subject was always presented with such a mystery that it made this whole business of love sound something like those low-flying white clouds that came over on clear days in June. They looked pretty and seemed almost close enough to touch, but they were always so flimsy and far away that a person could never really get to know what they were like.

This was the way Abe felt about his love for Mary Ruth. Everybody made love sound so untouchable and cloudy and complicated that Abe didn't know whether his simple and plain feelings were enough to qualify. But although there wasn't any deep mystery to the way he felt, he guessed he loved Mary Ruth.

He knew he liked her a lot. And she liked him. They enjoyed being with each other. That is why they got married in the first place. When Mary Ruth started going with Abe when they were both still young, she knew what she was getting into. For one thing, vocation wasn't even a decision, not for Abe. He was a farmer's son, the offspring of the soil; and the progress from farmer's son to farmer is always so gradual that nobody really notices it happening. But at Wheatheart it was almost inevitable, especially if the farmers were as successful as the Ericsons.

So Mary Ruth knew that when she married Abe, she married the farm. She also knew that if she competed with the farm for her man's attention and priority, she would always come out second best. So she didn't compete. She cooperated. She became a part of that which would demand first place or even the essence in her husband's life. She became a farmer's wife, and fulfilled her own expectations and dreams and hopes through the farm. Instead of that farm coming between them like an old-fashioned bundling board, it brought them even closer together, as both of them sought for the richness of life within the boundaries of the farm which served as the family nucleus.

As a farmer's wife, Mary Ruth surrendered any individual ambitions she might have once had. Or if she didn't surrender, at least she hid them so well that even she couldn't locate them except in the deepest moments of introspection early in the morning just before the rooster crowed when she was the only person in her world yet awake.

But the absence of individual ambitions didn't stop her, didn't dull her enthusiasm for life or her devotion to duty. As a farmer's wife, as Abe's wife, she had an outlet for both. She took care of the duties and pleasures with such an even spirit that even those who knew her best—her mother, mother-in-law, Brother Bob's wife, and a couple of friends from high school—even those people couldn't tell which was duty and which was pleasure. That is what Abe liked about her, the dependability and evenness, the simple pleasure she found in fulfilling duty.

She took care of the house, fixed the meals at regular times, and brought them to the field in the busy season. During times of emergency such as harvest and planting, she took care of the outside chores and ran errands.

She represented the farm and Abe in community affairs. She took the time to shop at both of the grocery stores just to keep both merchants happy; this also gave her an opportunity to check one cross section of the community against the other, since some of the townspeople shopped exclusively at one store. Mary Ruth bought the customary wedding, baby, and graduation gifts. She taught at Vacation Bible School every summer, even on those years when harvest was so early that it almost interfered. She went to the Women's Missionary Circle almost every week, although she was about the only woman there who either didn't have small children or a retired husband to give them reason for going. She visited the sick, and took her turn sitting up with people who needed help. And in late August, when the work was all done, she permitted herself to enjoy a short vacation with Abe to Colorado or somewhere cool. In the midst of all this, she found time to can, sew, decoupage, garden, grow flowers, and read a bit, mostly grocery store magazines which Abe couldn't understand, much less appreciate. But she also stopped by the public library occasionally and picked up one of those books Abe remembered teachers talking about but you never caught anybody reading—like *Moby Dick*, *Oliver Twist*, or something by Mark Twain which wasn't *Tom Sawyer* or even *Huckleberry Finn*.

Mary Ruth also went to the football games. She went before they were married, when Abe was still playing, and naturally she went after. She knew enough to remember who won and most of the time who scored; but other than that, Abe couldn't tell how much she really knew about football, about the game or the legend, or the dreams, past or future. It was just one of those things they couldn't talk about, regardless of how comfortable they grew together. It was too deep to be reached in words. You just had to understand it. So Abe prepared himself to live with the fact that he didn't know how much she knew. But that was all right. Everybody has to live with himself down deep where decisions and dreams are made. Secretly, Abe welcomed the privacy.

All in all, theirs was a good marriage, convenient, efficient, based on a strong dose of like and maybe even love. But now with Mary Ruth heavy with child, they faced their first real test.

Despite the fact that Abe had been a good biology student, and had understood the facts of the RH factor the doctor had mentioned when they applied for their marriage license, he had not understood it emotionally until Mary Ruth had a miscarriage during their third year of marriage. Abe was confused, trapped between his decency requiring him to sympathize with Mary Ruth during her pain and hurts, and his own aspirations. Abe wanted a legacy. By then, Billy Ray Jackson, Abe's best friend in high school, and a good tight end, already had a son, as did Chris Schmidtz, one of the tackles, and Scott Garland.

From the tractor seat, Abe's wandering subconscious was suddenly jarred into oblivion by another vagabond, a thistle. Celebrated in song and story, the thistle (or the tumbleweed as it is called by the transients) is the clown prince of the prairie, cursed and loved, damned for its prolificity, promiscuity, and viciousness, yet, cherished in nostalgia as an ominous, roving landmark. After long trips away to more scenic places, the natives knew they were coming home when they began to see thistles blowing across the fields and jamming the barbed wire fences, making them seem less lonely and austere. Thistles are not really ugly plants in the spring when they are young and green. Their color is a bit lighter than many of the other weeds and cultivated plants that contrast with the dirt to make a vast color board; but they grow everywhere, with no regard for climate, cultivation, or farming proficiency. With plows and subsoil sweeps, good farmers like Abe could conquer most illicit vegetation that would challenge their crops and reputations. But the thistle only thrived on their efforts. Its long wormy root would grow to moisture and cling for life as it wriggled free from the plowshares which would destroy it, waiting in victory until frost turned it into an ugly brown mass of vicious stickery bush, and the wind sent it on a romantic, undisciplined tour of the wheat fields and pastures, always reminding the farmers of their deep roots, and the resistance it took to survive on the prairie.

All morning, Abe had played games with the thistles. As his subconscious entertained him, his tractor-driving eye was concentrating on their jagged paths as they threatened him and his work. Finally, one found its mark. At first, Abe thought it would hit the tractor wheel and be crushed by the might of water-weighted rubber; but it missed, falling just behind, lodging momentarily in the hitching mechanism, then plunging straight back into the curled fingers of the rotary hoe. One whole section of the machine stopped rolling and instead dragged through the dirt, pushing an ever-increasing mound in front, and leaving in its wake a ditch that would be difficult to cross with the combine. Understandably disgruntled, Abe stopped the tractor and started the rather difficult journey to the ground. He was upset by the delay, the break in activity and thought, the disruption of the possibility of where he might have been had he not had to stop. But secretly, very secretly, because such thoughts on the surface would have brought him guilt, Abe welcomed the change in position and dreams.

He felt the cleanliness of the dirt as he pulled the mound from in front of his machinery and with his bare fingers worked his way, cautiously, to the stickery culprit who had impeded his journey. Finally, with a sudden yank, he wrested it free from the machine which held it firm and, holding it high in the wind, released it to pursue its journey, looking far worse for its ordeal with mechanized farming.

Still kneeling, wedged between the tractor and implement, Abe realized that he was not in a hurry anymore. Perhaps it was because the wind was not as fierce from this perspective as it was from the tractor seat. Or perhaps it was a combination of the sounds of the quiet purring of a good tractor engine muffled by a stiff breeze and the smells of diesel and fresh dirt and the warm feeling of prairie soil heaped about his knees and legs, but Abe felt like staying.

His mind was in the present now, and he focused it on Mary Ruth. He did not concentrate on or even visualize her face, features, or figure. Those things were too incidental. Instead, he identified with what he thought must be her fears right now. He fought against those thoughts, but he lost, and tears came to his chest. There, in that humble but magnificent tabernacle of dirt and wheat plants and open air, Abe decided to pray. It was an unusual procedure for him. Abe had something of an unrealized agreement with God. He feared formality, and he supposed that God didn't care much for it either; but he understood that sometimes things were formal, although he wasn't sure why. Thus, Abe prayed when he was called on. On Sunday mornings, he helped take the offering and Brother Bob would always call on one of the offering gatherers for prayer before the plates were passed. Abe's turn would come up about once a month that way. On rarer occasions on Sunday evening, when there weren't many there, Brother Bob would call on Abe to pray just before the sermon. Although his pre-sermon and pre-offering prayers sounded a lot alike and his voice trembled, he managed to fulfill his duty. Others in the church, like Mrs. Simpson, prayed more elaborately and more beautifully, but Abe was a native in the church and he realized that the people needed to hear from him occasionally. Like Brother Bob said, it gave the members comfort.

But Abe didn't engage in formality when he didn't have to. God knew that Abe wanted rain in the fall and dry weather in June, and God knew that Abe loved Wheatheart and living. So Abe didn't see much need in filling in all the details. God was busy too.

But there was something about this morning, this moment, that made Abe conscious of a presence that demanded recognition. There, kneeling in dirt of his possession, he felt so happy and so helpless; but it was a good helplessness. He knew he didn't have any control over Mary Ruth's situation. But he knew it didn't matter.

"God, be with Mary Ruth, and be with . . . be with Mary Ruth. Amen." It had the force of a Luther, the conviction of a Calvin, and the eloquence of a Wesley; and the answer was clear. Abe stood, went to the side of the tractor, switched off the engine, walked the few hundred yards to his pickup, and drove home to his wife who was in labor.

Hurrying into Fatherhood
1965

Abe found Mary Ruth in the bedroom where she was packing a small suitcase with nightgowns and the baby things she had received at the shower given her by the church women.

"I'm glad you're home. I don't think I could have made it till dinnertime." (In western Oklahoma, dinnertime comes at noon, regardless of the size of the meal.) Abe thought he noticed some fear in her voice, so he scanned her face for further verification.

"I was worried about you." On this occasion, that statement was not so awkward for Abe as it would have been under more normal circumstances.

"Why did you quit anyway? I really didn't expect you with the way it's blowing and all. Something break?"

How does one explain the mysteries of answered prayer mingled with the raw dreams of expected parenthood, even to his own wife who would at least not ridicule him and might even attempt to understand? Abe chose not to try. "I picked up a thistle in the hoe." During the six years they had been married, Mary Ruth had not worked in the fields except to bring dinner out at noon during harvest, so she would have forgotten that Abe's excuse was not sufficient. Besides, that kind of short answer statement, which included a name-dropping familiarity with a piece of equipment, was part of the romance of the male role. It implied that there was a chasm between what Abe did and the way Mary Ruth understood it, and that chasm was a natural device for keeping the men strong and the women awed.

Mary Ruth didn't appear particularly awed this time, though. In fact, she might have been playing a counter game. "I guess I will take these cloth diapers. I think the hospital uses those paper things, but I will need some real stuff to bring the baby home. Abe, do you think this little gown will be all right?" She held up a small yellow garment which her own mother had made especially for the occasion.

Abe's knowledge of high fashion was limited largely to the difference between OshKosh and TufNut overalls and the difference between a suspension and padded football helmet. Yet, he did know that yellow was the color of nonstatement—blue for boys and pink for girls and yellow if you don't want to think about the possibility that your firstborn might not be a boy. Right then, yellow suited Abe.

"Abe, I think I am about to have another one." Mary Ruth dropped the gown into the suitcase and gripped the back of a chair. Abe moved toward her, engulfed her in his arms and held her very close as the intensity of the pain built. Abe could read the anguish in her face, and he could almost experience the growing severity as she clasped her fingers about his upper arms and dug into his muscles with her nails. Abe was relieved when it was over and Mary Ruth went back to her packing.

But Abe wasn't that casual. "I'll get the car." he said as he left for the garage in a hurry. Abe's hurry was not a run, but it was a lot faster than walking. Very quickly he had Mary Ruth and the bag in the car and they were on their way to Wheatheart. He had made the trip thousands of times, but this time was distinctive, and he would remember it frequently in years to come, particularly the high winds that were carrying dirt. On the open road, the wind blew even harder. Dust churned and puffed all around them and brought the boundaries of the prairie in close so that the world seemed smaller than usual. Abe noticed the dirt and thistles collecting in the fence rows, the farmers streaking the landscape with their rotary hoes, the milk truck driving into the dairy, the propane truck delivering fuel to Arlo Ballew's house. He saw it but he couldn't experience it. The normal activity was going on, but Abe, native that he was, couldn't relate to it. He had experienced this feeling before—during his high school playing days when his father drove him into town for the games. He and his father and his mother would make the trip in silence, but with constantly moving eyes. They all were noticing, but the things they were noticing were not worth talking about, so they just didn't talk. That activity on the horizon constituted the sights and symbols of the very meaning of life, but at the moment they didn't seem important.

Artificiality pervaded the trip to the hospital. In places, driving was treacherous and demanded all of Abe's attention. Particularly at the crests of the hills, the blowing dirt was so thick and swift that he could not see the edges of the road or any obstacles which might have been in his path. But Abe knew the road, and he was able to manipulate by instinct when sight failed; so he was able to measure their progress in rhythm to Mary Ruth's pains. He wanted to help her, to reach out and touch her as if by his touch he could absorb some of this pain himself. He was stronger than Mary Ruth and more capable of handling pain. Years of head-on tackling practices and hot summer hours without water had given him a tolerance for it. But he didn't reach out; he didn't touch her; instead, he offered pleasant words of encouragement, and drove on, right up to the emergency door of the Wheatheart Community Hospital.

Abe hated hospitals. He accused the odors, but it was really the efficiency. When he lost control of a situation, he lost composure. As soon as they moved through the large, steel swinging doors of the emergency entrance, Mary Ruth was seized by two nursing assistants, young girls just out of high school working at the hospital until they got enough money together to go over to Alva to college, or until they got a marriage offer and could go home and make babies themselves. Abe doubted their competence, and his doubt was compounded by their efficiency. They assured him that old Doc Heimer was on his way over, and then disappeared with his wife in tow. Alone, Abe wound his way through the corridor to the waiting room and stayed there until the dust and the darkness it created forced the chickens and citizens of Wheatheart indoors.

It was a restless afternoon. For brief periods, he leafed through the back copies of *Successful Farming* magazine, some nearly four years old; but most of the time he stood at the large, double window which faced the highway and watched the human and natural events of one of the most significant dust storms in the history of western Oklahoma.

Abe watched the sky turn from a dusty blue to a darker red, as the local dirt worked its way into the atmosphere. The sky then turned from the red to gray, as foreign soil blown in from hundreds of miles away, some probably as far away as Kansas, captured the environment. At five minutes until two, the street lights came on, just as three school buses came down the highway, nearly two hours early. Cars moved infrequently back and forth through town. Occasionally, one would pull up to the hospital, and after a short delay, a door would spring open and the driver would rush the distance from the car to the door, aided by the wind blowing from the back. Abe knew each of these people, some very well, yet each conversation sounded like the one before it.

"Oh, hi, Abe."

"Hello, Arnold."

"Someone sick?"

"Nope. This is our big day."

With visible and verbal registration, "Oh. Hey, congratulations! How is she doing?"

"All right, I guess. They don't tell you nothing."

Condescendingly assuring, "Well, old Doc Heimer would let you know if there was anything to know."

"How about you? Visiting somebody?"

"Yeah, Charlie Bloom."

"Oh, what's wrong with him?"

"Gall bladder."

"Too bad, but this is as good a place as any to be on a day like this."

"Isn't that the truth. My windows and doors leaked so bad that I put sheets and blankets up. They help some, but dust is still getting through. I have never seen it this bad."

Every time Abe heard that, he remembered that in their haste, they had not made temporary barricades against the torments of nature. He remembered with a knot in his stomach, because as much as he disliked this hospital, he dreaded going home.

"Well, good luck, Abe. I hope she gets along all right. What do you want, boy or girl?"

"It doesn't matter, as long as it's healthy." There is a difference between ritual and a lie, and these people did not want the truth. Besides, the truth would require an explanation, and neither of them had time for that.

"That's good. I am sure it will be. Call me if you need any help. We're always around the place somewhere." Some of that was ritual too, but as a native, Abe knew the difference.

"Thanks. I'll do that." And Abe went back to his watching.

But it was more than watching. He was watching the present from the caverns of remembering, restless remembering. Unlike the tractor-driving remembering, which could grab an image and hold on to it through to conclusion, this remembering only flitted around Doc Heimer and the hospital; but during the afternoon, that core extended itself to incorporate nearly everyone Abe had ever known and nearly every year of his life.

Doc Heimer was one of the most dependable permanents in Wheatheart. He had been a vital part of the community as long as Abe could remember. He delivered Abe, took his tonsils out, sutured his boyhood nicks, wormed him, gave him his football physicals, and set his arm when he broke it the last game of his sophomore year. He used to practice in an old office with a few hospital beds just above the drugstore. The office window faced Main Street, and the metal awning that separated his window from the drugstore plate glass front below was covered with layers of tobacco juice collected from years of the one habit that gave the Doc identity with the working class. When the scientific age finally enveloped Wheatheart, the citizens conducted a fundraising and managed enough to build the new hospital and buy Doc a new Ford, both of which he drove casually and completely.

Being the only doctor in town is not an easy life, but Doc managed to see every football game. He stood on the sideline, spit tobacco juice on the yard markers, yelled at the officials, and checked the players for dilated pupils and swollen knees. Although Abe had never been hurt badly enough to require Doc's services, except for the broken arm he got making the tackle during the second half kick-off of the state semifinal game with Blanchard in his sophomore year, he appreciated Doc's uncanny ability to get a player repaired and back into the flow of the season as quickly as possible. That proved two things, loyalty and medical brilliance. A lesser doctor or a lesser man could not have done it.

It was good that Doc should have this hospital and that Mary Ruth should be getting his attention.

Although the sun had completely disappeared before noon and the street lights had burned through the dusty darkness since two o'clock, Abe knew when dusk came. Usually, this time of day would have spawned a restlessness in him, because it was chore time. On normal days, this restlessness would have disturbed him into completing his business and getting home as quickly as possible, particularly if Mary Ruth were with him. All his adult life, Abe had envied people with teenage children, especially sons, who could relax at dusk because they had help with chores.

But Abe today was neither restless nor disturbed, as he waited by the window. This was a different day. Not doing your chores twice each day is an oversight tantamount to criminal negligence, completely out of character for a good farmer, but today Abe had forgotten the code.

He heard footsteps in the corridor and turned to see Doc come through the swinging doors which separated the hospital business from the visitors. He was dressed in the white efficiency which would have frightened Abe, had it not been for beard stubble and yellow teeth that shone above his pulled-down surgical mask and gave identification with the practical world.

"It's a boy, Abe. A boy. Mary Ruth's got a little boy." He talked fast, and sounded almost enthusiastic.

Abe didn't know whether to be happy, surprised, or simply calm. He decided that an "I told you so," attitude might be out of place. "A boy! Are you sure?"

"Unless they changed the model without telling me."

"Doc, you're sure?"

"Now, Abe, I have been delivering babies for a long time, and I tell you, you got a boy."

That was enough of that game. He wasn't very good at it anyway. "Thanks, Doc."

"He's a good-looking boy, Abe. We just got him, and they're still cleaning him up some, but he looks healthy and strong. You sure must be proud."

"Well, I don't know. I haven't seen him yet. How's Mary Ruth?"

"She's a little groggy, but both of them will be ready for you in a few minutes."

"Thanks, Doc." Abe realized that he had said that before, but words were elusive at a time like this.

"Well, Abe. I can tell you now that I sure am relieved. We have been pretty cautious throughout this whole thing. I know how important a baby was to you all. Mary Ruth did a good job."

"She's a good woman, Doc." Abe had never said that to anyone in his life, and he couldn't remember ever having thought about it before.

"Abe, I don't want to worry you, but there is something we

might ought to talk about." This was out of character too, because Doc Heimer had developed his personality to fit his blunt bedside manner. Maybe Abe's confession had startled him. "Sometimes these babies from RH parents have to have blood transfusions."

"What do you mean, Doc? Doesn't he have enough blood?" Abe's enthusiasm was turning into fright and his fright into anger directed toward no one in particular.

"Oh, they have plenty of blood, but it is the wrong kind. We have to drain out the old and put in some new."

"What?"

"Well, it's like changing oil in that old diesel John Deere out there. When the old oil wears out and the tractor can't run, you drain it out, put the plug back in, and fill it up with new stuff. Well, we may have to do that with your boy, Abe. It is just about like changing oil in the tractor. You may have to take him down to Oklahoma City where they have access to the blood bank, but it is a rather common thing and perfectly safe."

"When would we have to do this?"

"Well, not tonight. You go home and get some sleep; then get back up here early in the morning and we'll see if the symptoms develop during the night."

Abe interrupted, "Doc, how will we know . . . how will we know whose blood they put into him?"

"Well, they figure out what blood type he needs and they just get that type out of the bank. Everything is really scientific these days. There isn't any guesswork in this at all."

"No, I mean, well, how will we know whose blood it is?"

Doc either didn't hear the question or chose not to answer it. "They have blood in jars, Abe, with the type marked on them. They won't make a mistake."

"But, Doc, what will happen to the blood he has now? Oh, well, I guess it isn't important. If this is what we have to do, we have to do it."

"Nothing to worry about. It's perfectly safe. You won't be gone more than a day. Now, you call your folks and then you can go in and see Mary Ruth before you go home. Do you need any pills for tonight?"

"Naw." Abe was amused at the thought.

"I didn't figure you would. Other people do, though. You'd be surprised," and Doc started back through the doors of mystery. "Oh, by the way, Abe, make those gals back in the nursery hold that boy up for you. They'll spoil him for sure anyway, and you may as well get in on the fun."

There was no way that Abe could analyze or store all of the emotions and thoughts and feelings which deserved his attention. They stormed around each other in such a way that they neutralized and canceled, until the whole event seemed artificial. Perhaps that is the difficulty with being so attached to the past. The mind is not ready for a multileveled present. But in those times, Abe knew enough of Wheatheart and its manners to find stability in custom; so he went to the pay phone, dug two dimes from his overall pocket, and called his folks, and then Mary Ruth's.

"Hello?" Most area women still answered the phone with a high shrill voice reminiscent of the days when they had to shout to be heard and telephone messages only brought bad news. Good equipment and underground lines had not only long ago corrected the technical difficulties, but now the better machines coupled with the coming of spare time into the rural woman's life had made the phone the village news media. But the greeting was traditional.

"Mom."

"Abe, we have been worried about you. We have been trying to call out to your place all afternoon, and we never did get anybody. Is anything wrong?" Abe's parents had moved to town when he and Mary Ruth got married, but they still checked the events of the old home place daily.

"Mom, the baby came. We got a boy."

"A boy!" Her exclamation was followed by a shout into the distance, "James, Abe and Mary Ruth got a baby. Abe, how big is he?" Abe never understood the meaning of that question, but it was part of the custom.

"I don't know. They are just cleaning him up now."

"How's Mary Ruth? She make it all right?"

"Yeah. Doc said she was fine."

"What are you going to call the boy, Abe?" Mothers don't waste much time.

"Jimmy Charles."

"How nice. After his two grandpas."

"Mom." He tried to become serious.

"Yes?"

"Doc says we may have to change his blood."

"Well, I knew they were doing that now." Rural women also practiced a lot of medicine with the aid of farm publications and weekly newspapers, and Abe's mom would have anticipated him.

"But, Mom," and Abe decided she wouldn't understand either.

Nevertheless, he was her son and she heard the apprehension. "Now, Abe, you have known Doc too long to feel like that. Doc knows best and if he says that is what you have to do, then that is what you have to do."

"I think I will stay in town tonight."

"It's probably best. I'll make the bed for you. You been gone all day?"

"We left right before dinner."

"Were you blowing?"

"Well, the home place wasn't too bad when we left, but I had to work the Cole place this morning."

"I figured you would. That's all that old place is good for. You come on by when you get ready. I'll scrape up something for you to eat. Your dad and I can go out in the morning and get the dirt out of your house."

"Bye."

Abe used his other dime to call Mary Ruth's mother. Since this was not their first grandchild, she was not as enthusiastic nor as inquisitive, but she did volunteer to do the chores which Abe had forgotten. Abe might have had a hard time communicating with Mary Ruth's folks, but they surely were helpful.

Abe timed his phone calls perfectly because as he hung up the phone, the young nurse appeared at the swinging door and invited him into the sterile region.

Abe wanted to peek through the plate glass front of the nursery window, but there was too much efficiency at the moment, so he went directly to Mary Ruth's room. She looked haggard but managed a smile.

Abe realized that he had to carry most of the conversation. "How do you feel?"

"Happy and hurting."

"I feel a little that way myself just now." The thought of the transfusion haunted him still.

"I think those are called sympathy pains." She didn't understand his thoughts, but perhaps she didn't know yet.

"Doc says you did just fine."

"I'll take his word for it. I guess I know now what it's like to buck hay bales in 110 degrees."

"Are we still agreed on Jimmy Charles?"

"Sure."

"Mary Ruth," he paused to grasp his utterance and decided against it. "I'll see you early in the morning."

She reached for his hand. "Abe, things are going to be like we both want them to be."

Abe bent down and kissed her. Despite that distinctive hospital smell that enveloped her and the entire situation, it was a pleasant sensation, and Abe was sincere. "I'll be up early."

By design, Abe approached the nursery in a burst. He walked parallel to the window with his eyes focused on the "Exit" sign in the hallway as long as his anticipation would permit him, but as soon as he knew that he was even with the window and the activities and life within, he exploded into perpendicularity. There was Jimmy Charles, his Jimmy Charles, nestled in the arm of one of the young nurses, looking so weak and alive and red and wonderful. Though no sound came from the heavily constructed and cushioned nursery, his crying was conspicuous. His mouth was opened wide and trembling, his forehead wrinkled into consternation, and his small chest vibrated as he sucked in a gust of air to fortify his defiance of the world outside the womb. And he flailed his limbs—all of them. Arms and fingers and legs and toes were constant movement, making creative patterns in the space allowed him by the nurse's body. He was dressed only in a diaper so fatherhood could assess the near totality of creation, unrestricted and unencumbered.

Abe liked it. He could have stayed there, glued to that satisfaction, all evening or forever. Through the births and deaths of animals, and of relatives and neighbors, Abe had never taken life for granted, but he had never fully known what it was until now. Just to verify the moment, he tried on the name—Jimmy Charles, Abe Ericson's boy—and the appellation rang as crisp and clear as an October night, and laid the dust of this stormy day.

Abe returned the smiles of the nurse, who was obviously tiring of her duties of display, and walked slowly toward the emergency exit. As he stepped through the door, he was slapped with the winds of the present and he instantly reviewed the day. His mind, in a fleeting moment rested on that thistle which had balled up his hoe, and he remembered the words of his prayer. Without bowing his head, without taking his eyes off the purpose of walking toward his car, he said, in a mental shout, "Dear Father, thanks," and he knew then that everything would be all right.

The next morning when Abe pulled into the hospital parking lot just before six, the ambulance was already parked outside. He knew what it was there for without asking, but Doc Heimer met him in the hall and confirmed it.

"I was going to call you, but Mary Ruth said you would be here early."

"Yeah. What's the problem?" and he wondered if Doc ever slept. Farm folks get up early as part of the code, but what was Doc's code?

"Just as we thought. We will have to do the blood change.

They're expecting you in at St. Anthony in the City. I called the ambulance because it can go faster if it needs to, and the baby may need some oxygen or something. One of the nurses will go along with you so you won't have the burden on yourself. I have found after all these years that new fathers are pretty darn worthless when it comes to baby care." Abe didn't bristle at that. In fact, he felt worthless and there wasn't any need to fake a mood.

"Thanks, Doc. Is it all right if I go along for the ride?"

"Oh sure. Catch the big city life. This may be the last time, now that you have family responsibilities." Doc knew the words of Wheatheart, but sometimes one would get the impression that he might be using them more to chide than to communicate.

Abe interrupted Mary Ruth's breakfast only briefly, and armed with her admonition to take care of Jimmy Charles, he got in the ambulance and sat down beside that young nurse who looked even younger and more unsure as she held his posterity. It was almost a tragic sight, helplessness being held by fragility, and Abe spent the first ten miles of the trip studying his hands—large by genetics, stained from the grease and oil of farm repair, calloused and scarred from hours of virile labor, leathered by days and months of exposure to sun and cold, and awkward by comparison with his present surroundings.

Contrasts are commonplace for the Oklahoma farmers, with the weather always setting the tempo. This day was as pure as yesterday was vulgar. The sun illuminated the colors. Now that the loose dust had been blown away by yesterday's wind, the wheat was green with promise, the soil was red with stability, sprigs of new grass dotted the brown pastures and a few red buds were just beginning to speck the brush. The thistles and blow-sand seemed comfortable in their new homes in the fence rows and lay quietly and perfectly calm as if someone had arranged them as a model for a still-life drawing.

But the trip wasn't quiet. The ambulance was filled with crying that was, in turn, plaintive, dismal, demanding, and torturous. Jimmy Charles was not happy, and his immediate world was not happy as a result. The nurse, obviously limited in her knowledge and experience, tried everything she knew. She held him close; rocked him, sang to him, alternately tried feeding and burping, but all to no avail. The torrents were interrupted only to allow him to rest his shoulders and gather more wind for the next gust. Abe volunteered his hands, and she agreed in surrender. She showed him how, the exchange was made, and the crying stopped. That might have been the biggest moment in Abe's life since the first time he put on the Whippet game uniform back in the seventh grade, except that it was temporary, abruptly temporary. Jimmy Charles dried the wellspring long enough to rest his lungs and then began again. Father, nurse, and driver rejoiced to see the City and the thought of peace it would bring.

Abe was even more uncomfortable in this hospital than he was in Wheatheart Community. The nuns were not only efficient, they were austere as well. At least, that is the way he thought they would be, so that is the way they became, even though he was surprised by the smiling eyes he thought he detected. Besides that, he was bothered by the little statues that decorated the alcoves in the halls. He didn't know what they were for, but they reminded him of something very old and very foreign, and he knew they possessed a mysteriousness he couldn't understand. He tried reading the names of some and discovered that they were the same names he had heard in Sunday School all his life—Peter, Paul, John, Luke, distinguished from his religious world by that everpresent title, St. Even the young nurse from home was a welcome sight when she emerged in her white friendliness from behind the swinging doors and told him that since it would be about six hours, he might as well go downtown or something. He took her advice.

For Abe, Oklahoma City was not a real city like the other cities in the country. It was another town, like Wheatheart except bigger. It was where you went when you sold cattle or went to the fair, and in those places you met people just like yourself, farm people, who had come to the City to meet other farm people. They were in the City, but they hadn't left their codes or their language or their roots. But there were City people too, and they were worth studying. Abe found a bench near a downtown drugstore and spent most of the day just sitting. This was the first time he had ever had so much free time in the City, so he impatiently enjoyed the wait. Sometimes, the flood of people almost engulfed him as he tried to study each, the mood, carriage, and dress; when that happened, he would retouch reality by wondering if these people would care that he had a new son. If he had been a man of fulfilled impulse, he would have shouted it out loud, so everyone could rejoice; but being silent and smug had its rewards too.

But even the crowd could not wall in his remembering the past and the future. He had to remember quickly, because he was also watching the passersby with the intensity of a stranger in a foreign world. But he could remember—and experience—the back rushing through an almost nonexistent hole for a necessary first down, the quarterback launching a thirty-yard bullet right on target, an intercepted pass, a recovered fumble, a blocked kick, a victory handshake, and the crying. Each time the crying of the morning crowded into the images and interrupted them and chased them away. Was he prepared for fatherhood? Did he understand? Could there really be something wrong with his son? But that thought didn't belong with the rest of them and he obliterated it by returning to his people-watching.

About an hour before the time he was expected back at the hospital, his remembering took a more concrete direction, and he began to search the downtown streets for a familiar place. He knew it was just a block off Main Street, somewhere on one of the side streets, so he looked from that perspective until he discovered the sign, just as he had remembered it from the time he had been here during high school days—Chuck's Sporting Goods. He walked in and invested $23 (that was nearly fifteen bushels of wheat) in the finest football they had in stock. He was ready to go home.

To complete the day, the trip home was a contrast. Jimmy Charles alternated his time between Abe's and the nurse's arms and between sleeping peacefully and lying awake contentedly. Not once did he cry or even whimper, not even when the exchanges were made. The nurse was too young to understand all this contrast, and just as they pulled across the tracks on the outskirts of Wheatheart, she remarked, "I can't believe how quiet he's been. It's almost as if it is another baby."

Abe hated her for that statement, and he never forgot it. But life and infancy is too short to worry too long about absurd things, and with that semiassurance, he hurried into fatherhood.

To Raise a Good Son
1965

From her hospital bed, Mary Ruth took care of the formal announcements. From his pickup truck along Main Street, Abe took care of the informal ones. Because of the weather change, he had the time to do it, and the local folk had the time to listen.

After his trip to Oklahoma City, Abe went home to find that his tractor and rotary hoe had been returned to the barn; (although not quite in the proper place, the equipment was, nonetheless, in the barn), the chores had been done ritualistically, and the kitchen table had been loaded with dishes of precooked foods awaiting only final heating or cold enjoyment. If a transient had checked the bottoms of the casserole pots, the plastic containers, or the pie plates which housed those delicacies, he would have been able to call the roll of the neighborhood. But Abe was a native; and for most of the dishes, he didn't have to check the bottoms. He could identify the food. He had been to enough potluck suppers, wedding receptions, and post-funeral dinners to know the culinary speciality of nearly every lady in the Wheatheart area; and he occasionally found himself anticipating the next event with tastes of some particular recipe locked in his memory.

He paid tribute to each cook as he carefully put the food away—
Mrs. Bryant's spinach casserole, Bertha Ogden's chicken and dumplings, Louise Smith's currant pie, Fern Walker's watermelon pickles,
Bessie Meyer's chocolate cake, and Grandma Reinschmidt's home-
made bread.

With only hints of guilt, he sampled a bit of each with the same
fork, and went to bed. When he awoke the next morning, it was
raining.

Rain always comes unexpectedly in western Oklahoma. After days
and weeks and months of forecasting (both professional and ama-
teur), expectations, planning, pessimism, cursing and praying, the
rains come, and the drought ends. Sometimes the rains come like a
temper tantrum, an emotional burst from bitter, angry clouds which
have accumulated, turned black, and hung dormant along the south-
western horizon. Sometimes the rains come like Johnny Apple-
seed—dancing, skipping, and flinging scattered life around the area
with no pattern or consistency.

Sometimes the rains come like smiles from gentle angels. The
whole upperworld turns to a beautiful, nondescript gray; and with a
gentleness that could only be written by a caring Cause, the drops
flow slowly, steadily, and universally. With purpose, the premium
moisture seeks out the parched soil and trickles through the dirt
pebbles, mingling between the shoots of the vegetation and scam-
pering underground to its watery mission. This was the kind of
unexpected blessing Abe woke to.

He hurried through his chores with thoughts of what a lucky man
he was. He had a new life to advertise and now the weather would
provide him with an audience. Abe especially enjoyed going to town
on rainy days for there was always a spirit of unhurried purpose.
Town would be filled with pickups and cars vying for the parking
spaces along Main Street and in front of the grocery stores. Farm
folks chose non-workdays to accomplish necessary shopping; they
could take their time, and the merchants profited. Rain meant extra
bushels of wheat at harvest, and extra bushels meant extra money.
Husbands and wives would talk about a new coat for Betty Jean, an

extra milk bucket, a chain saw, a new set of tires for the car, or some luxury which had lain silent in thought until the rain brought germination. On rainy days, and particularly on these kinds of rainy days, they usually bought.

When people bought, they also talked. They would meet at the drugstore or huddle under a canopy and talk of rain, wheat prices, deaths, and of new babies.

Abe directed his pickup truck and his opening announcement to his favorite store, the John Deere place, owned by the Garlands. The Garland family had been prominent in the Wheatheart area ever since statehood days when Josiah Garland had migrated in from Illinois and set up a blacksmith shop and wagon store. Through hard work and a reputation for honesty and concern, he kept up with progress of the town and technology, moved into the implement and tractor business sometime during the thirties, and through an amazing run of good luck during the war was able to keep his customers supplied with most of their equipment necessities. Machinery was expensive during those war years, but at least it was available. His son Art, the first all-state football player in Wheatheart history, took over the management in the fifties, and built the company into one of the leading John Deere agencies in the area. During those years, the store also became a daytime community center. Now Art shared the fun of operation and the profits with his two sons, Scott and Chuck, both alumni of the high school and local football.

Although it was still early, the community meeting was in full discussion when Abe got there. Art and Scott Garland rested in the tilted desk chairs in the isolated office cubicles while a gathering of the prosperous and the struggling huddled around, some standing and some sitting on five-gallon buckets of oil, cardboard cases, and old tractor seats assembled for that purpose. Although the tone of the conversation revealed no pecking order, and a transient could not have distinguished the prosperous from the struggling, there was a definite hierarchy; and Abe, knowing his place, slid in comfortably.

Charlie Brady was in the midst of his drunk steer story. Abe had heard it before many times, as had the others, but Charlie needed to tell it once more. The story probably wasn't true, but frequent telling gave it credibility in Charlie's mind, and it was an important story to keep in the folk-legend catalog. "We had that silage, corn it was, stored for more than three years. We just threw it out to those old calves and they got higher'n a kite, just laid around and bellerd. That's all they did all day." The story became increasingly amusing to Charlie; but for the others, enjoyment was only polite.

Art Garland recognized Abe first. Since he had heard Charlie's story before, he felt he could interrupt it, and besides, Art Garland could interrupt the conversation any time he chose to. "Hi, Abe. Come into town to trade off your old combine now that you got all that moisture out there?" Art was a friendly man, but he also sold machinery. Sometimes Abe couldn't tell the difference. And he suddenly realized that he did need to buy something while he was there.

"Nope. Won't make a lot of difference if the wheat does make, with prices what they are. You still can't make any money in this business. I just came to buy sickle sections. I'll just patch up and get by again this year." Two things keep farmers from wealth, water and Washington; and the code required complaining about whichever was in season.

Oscar Bryant, a big farmer out by the river, acknowledged Abe's youthful wisdom. "Ain't it the truth! Wheat went down again yesterday. We're farming below cost now." He had just bought two new tractors with cabs.

Another asked, "How much is it today?"

From the crowd, "Two dollars two bits in Kansas City."

A consensus summary, "I can't believe that it is less than fifteen years ago and the price of diesel has doubled." Of course, tractors and plows and combines—the machines in the building—had doubled in price; but since that wasn't the Garlands' fault, those things were omitted from the inventory.

Someone else added to the list, "And what about the price of land? Did you hear what the old Wright place brought last week?" Everybody knew. That kind of information spreads as quick as national news and is more pertinent; but the speaker continued, "$65,000 for an old wheat quarter."

R.B. Jackson, who played tight end on the championship team of 1948, was always empirically practical. He asked, "How many bushels of wheat is that at two bucks two bits? Figure that out for us, Scott. You got an adding machine." It was more of a frustrated threat than command, and Scott responded as such. Then R.B. added in finality, "It'll never pay. Never. You just can't farm that much out of a quarter section."

By that time, Charlie Brady was at the eruption stage. "Yep. You young fellars about to learn somthun. You betcha. She can get worse. Believe me. I seen her worse. So has Art. We don't get these politics straightened out, we can get another depression and then there we are. Just like the old days. Ask Art. He remembers. You young fellars got all that money borrowed, living like there ain't no tomorrow. Well, let me tell you what rough is. We didn't have nothun. Oh, we made pretty good wheat, but didn't do any good. Couldn't sell it. Nobody had any money. Roosevelt got to be President and he paid us to plow her up. Sure did. Plowed up good wheat, but then we made some money next year."

Everybody had heard his story before, and Charlie knew that; but he had a commitment to keep some sanity in the neighborhood. "I fed my family and stock working for the W.P.A. I worked out on that overpass out by the cemetery. Me and a team of old mules I had. Dollar and half a day for me and the team. And those were big days. No coffee breaks back then. Hauled all that dirt in there with a slip. Built that overpass, but we kept food on the table. That's more than a lot of people did." Staying off soup lines in the early thirties was one of Charlie's biggest accomplishments. He went to school before they played football.

Scott Garland had a duty to the group and to himself to change the conversation. "Yeah, Charlie. You W.P.A. boys did a lot of good around town. But I wish you would go out and get your name off the sidewalk out there. It makes everybody think this is a depression outfit."

Charlie realized this as the termination to his speech, but he needed one final jolt. "That's good for you. Make you remember what hard times are all about. You would be wise to go out there and look at that once in a while just so you won't forget."

As they were shifting their minds for more pleasant thoughts to throw into the discussion, it was Art who remembered Abe's purpose. "By the way, Abe, I guess congratulations are in order. Where are the cigars?"

Abe had waited a long time for this and had listened to a lot of Charlie Brady stories. For at least nine months, he had rehearsed this scene from the tractor seat and other settings of introspection. He had burned with readiness through the drunk steers and the depression, and he had his moment.

He grinned, reached into his bib pocket, pulled out a handful of cigars which had grown only partially stale from waiting as long as he had. And then Abe became eloquent, "Here, have one." Things never go the way they are planned; and in retrospection, he would have done it differently, but he was satisfied with the outcome.

He distributed the cigars person to person and received the congratulations and the thanks. Joe Wells contributed the opening line. "It's a boy, I heard, Abe."

"Yep." He was still eloquent.

Another asked, "What's his name, Abe?"

"Jimmy Charles."

Someone in the crowd acknowledged, "Sure, that figures."

Scott Garland phrased the significant question. "Well, does he look like a pulling guard?" Scott had never played anything but quarterback, and since his career paralleled Abe's, the name of Ericson would always be a name for a pulling guard, perhaps a good pulling guard, but always a pulling guard. Abe's stomach developed a sudden ache that swept up through his heart and into his throat and eyes. It was a familiar pain. He first encountered it the first day of practice during the seventh grade when Coach Rambo had told him that he was a lineman, but after that he experienced it frequently—every time Scott made a long run or threw a pass, every time the newspaper or the John Deere conversation turned to the topic of football, every time he tried and failed to outrun Scott in wind sprints at the end of practice. All his football life, Abe had worked harder than Scott, had made fewer mistakes, had been more willing and had always been slower and less spectacular. But to the coaches, to Scott and to the community, he was a pulling guard; and now this had become his legacy. He remembered a Bible verse from a Brother Bob sermon about the sins of the father visiting the children, but his dreams would not permit him to dwell on that.

"He's got a fullback's chest."

R.B. Jackson was practical again. "But does he have a hollow head?" Everyone laughed. Although some were probably offended by the remark, R.B. had been too good an end for them not to laugh. "Do you remember that big old Laubach that was all-state at Waynoka?" He was grabbing a 1948 illustration from fifteen years of football history, but they all remembered. "That was the dumbest guy I ever saw. I'll never forget the coin toss." R.B. was the captain, but everyone remembered that too. "He said, 'Jackson, I'm going to hit you tonight.' And did he ever! Once he bit me in the pile. But he was a good fullback."

Someone affirmed that statement, "Best I ever saw."

Scott changed the era. "Well, I don't know. When we played Temple our junior year, they had a good one. I can't remember his name, but he sure ran with his knees high. Way up in the air, and he had good speed. You remember him, Abe?"

Abe remembered him. He remembered that the good back was the middle linebacker on defense, and he remembered blocking him so that Scott could option around the right end for twelve yards and the touchdown to win the game. Abe remembered better than Scott did, but he couldn't make an issue of it.

Someone from the crowd changed the era. "Yeah, but I still think the best runner I ever saw was that little kid from Woodward. He had more speed than anyone we have ever had out in this country, and he had real smooth moves. Nothing jerky about his cuts."

Another confirmed it, "And he could catch the ball too. Best pair of hands I've seen."

Art Garland brought the discussion back to Abe's immediacy, "Well, I wouldn't say that. That Earl Harding caught everything Scott ever threw to him." Earl had been a transient who had played for Wheatheart during Abe's sophomore and junior years. After that he disappeared and no one had heard from him, except there had been some rumors that he might have gone to junior college in Kansas. "That ball he caught against Lone Wolf was the best catch I ever saw. He just reached up and grabbed it with one hand. Took it right out of the defender's arms. I thought it was intercepted until he caught it."

With that prick of recollection, every man in the store relived the play in all its color—everyone except Abe. Abe remembered the play as well as the others. In fact, he had heard it described so often, he could visualize it as if he had seen it; but when Earl actually caught the ball, Abe had been busy trying to block a persistent defensive end who had greatly altered Scott's throwing rhythm that night. On that particular play, Abe had utilized a rolling block, sacrificing his body by throwing himself at the knees of the onrush. When the collision came, there was a dull impact on the ribs and the kidneys; but a brightness in the heart of competition because the big end came down, sprawling on the ground, and he too missed the spectacular catch. The others remembered the play, but Abe—and perhaps that big end—remembered only the block.

With the dexterity of a broken field runner in open space, the rainy morning football conversation darted from era to era, from skill to skill, from team to team, and from position to position; and all morning Abe stood mostly mute and witnessed the parade from the anonymity of a pulling guard. But the pain of that perspective was not as sharp as it had been in all the times before. This morning there was possibility—the therapeutic antidote of the future. Now he had a son.

After the conversation at the John Deere store, Abe had gained enough confidence to work his way up Main Street announcing the news in several stores, both the permanents and the transients. Although the conversations might have sounded the same to an outside eavesdropper, they were different. In each place, Abe catalogued specific variations to be called up again on the next dusty day he had to make swaths across a blowing field.

With such an important piece of news to spread, Abe would have been allowed some leeway with the rituals, but he chose not to take any. He was a native and he would observe the ageless standards to the letter of the legend. Thus, he drove. Half-block by half-block he moved his pickup and himself up Main Street, stopping in stores he visited regularly and only on special occasions. But each time he honored the pickup protocol which says that a prairie farmer should never be separated from his machine. This day, he could have walked, he could have run, he could have sprinted like a halfback in open field. He could have danced on the clouds which brought the rain and the promise, but he didn't. Driving was his pledge of good faith, his vote of confidence in this, his town. It was almost a sacrifice. He had a son to announce. But that news, that announcement, had to be made within the spirit of the community itself.

The first stop was at the gift shop operated by Carl and Helen Bledsoe, transients who had come into town after retiring from one of the branches of the military. Abe couldn't remember which one, but he knew it had something to do with the ocean and ships.

"Hi, Abe." Carl Bledsoe, though a transient, had fitted in nicely. Not only was he a regular at all the games and a soft touch for cheerleader buttons, but on occasions he had even joined the birddogs along the sidelines. He didn't know much about soil, and he had even been heard once complaining about government subsidies to farmers. Still, he was accepted, and people stopped in his store for cards or for a gift when a fancy relative was getting married in Wichita or somewhere.

"Hi. How's business?" Abe had news, but small talk always came first.

"Well, the rain sure brought a lot of traffic to town. Doesn't make a lot of difference to us though. We just get by in the fall and wait for spring to come.''

"Why, that's like a wheat farmer—harvest once a year.'' Abe had never though of it before, but he was happy he did now. He thought he detected a smile of acceptance in Carl's face when he heard that.

"Sure enough. Just like you wheat farmers. And if it doesn't rain, we don't get much harvest either.''

"Well, I wouldn't think that. It seems to me that people have to get born and die, whether it rains or not.''

"Yeah. You would think that all right, but you would be surprised. I sometimes get the idea that you wheat farmers are so tough that you don't even cash in except during good times.'' His lips didn't laugh but his eyes did, so Abe picked up the cue.

"Well, the cemetery is on a rise out there, and that clay sure gets hard in dry times.''

"Just being neighborly, eh.'' With this they both chuckled, and an outsider might have thought that they had something in common.

"By the way,'' Abe couldn't be caught enjoying this conversation too long. He had several stores to visit. "Do you have any of those little cards where you can write notes on?'' He made a picture with his thumb and forefinger just in case Carl couldn't understand the words.

"Sure. Thank-you notes for Mary Ruth, I betcha. Got 'em in bunches right over there in that glass case. Just help yourself there. And congratulations. I heard all about that boy. In fact, if you want my opinion,'' and at this point Abe was having so much fun that he really was interested in Carl's opinion, "she ought to make *you* write all those notes. After all, it is your boy. You're the one that's going to get all the benefit of watching him carry that football up and down the field.''

He was teasing, but Abe couldn't tell how much. Perhaps this man with clean fingernails and a white shirt could see things too. All of a sudden, Abe realized that it didn't make Carl Bledsoe a lot of difference that Abe had been a pulling guard, and he had to stop short to keep from appreciating that fresh perspective. Years later, when Abe recalled buying those thank-you notes, he had to argue with himself to keep from liking Carl Bledsoe, a transient, more than he should. This was just a good time, something for the moment, to be laughed at now but never to be placed along side the permanent.

Carl interrupted Abe's conflict before it could mature. "Bought him a ball yet?"

Abe grinned. It was a lucky guess, but Carl did understand some things.

Carl read the grin. "Going to make him carry it when he drives the tractor so he will learn not to drop it?"

Abe laughed only politely now. That last statement was too wild. No native, no one who understood, would have said that. Carl was what he was, a retired military man from one of those branches out in California who had moved to Wheatheart just to get away from the crowd. If he said the right things, it was only because he was trying to get the business.

Abe paid and left, still working his way up Main Street, taking his pickup as he went, and he wondered that day and during those days to come if Carl Bledsoe made fun of that custom too.

By noon, he had worked his way to the Dew Drop Inn where the conversation was like that of the John Deere place, except louder, faster, and more scattered. The cafe society was more cosmopolitan. The farmers in bib overalls and fertilizer caps mingled with the telephone and electric linemen in muddy boots and hard hats. Main Street proprietors and grain-elevator employees came to agitate and referee when the discussion left football and turned to some divided issue, such as all unions versus the Farmers Union.

Here the congratulations were less genuine, but the cigars more appreciated. Although he always experienced remote pangs of guilt every time he ate in a restaurant, Abe reasoned that it was better to stay in town for an afternoon visit to the hospital; and he was enjoying the conversation and the rain. He just hoped that none of those dear ladies who had helped stock his kitchen table with provisions would see him eating cafe food instead of something nourishing and tasty. But the mission was worth the danger.

After the Main Street tour and shopping spree ended, Abe spent a slow afternoon at the hospital. He managed to wade through the foreboding odor and order long enough to maintain a feeling of belonging. He shared his day between sitting in Mary Ruth's room and standing in front of the plate glass nursery room window which exhibited his lineage to the world.

As Abe had known him in his memory and dreams, Jimmy Charles was good. He lay pleasantly, explored space with his limbs, and tried to master the art of seeing; but he never cried or whimpered. Abe enjoyed watching him, even when no one else was there.

Mary Ruth was not so restful. Abe was content to help her watch it rain, but she had an obligation to get the announcement cards to friends and relatives. So they spent the afternoon listing cousins, aunts, uncles, second cousins, and fellow graduates who had moved away since high school. It was important to Mary Ruth to get a message to her friends, those girls who had chosen college instead of Wheatheart and were now married to coaches or assistant discount store managers and lived in such faraway places as El Reno or Claremore or Poteau. Although he mildly mocked the activity, Abe was glad for it. He wanted those people to know, to know that his dreams had taken flesh; and he wanted to go to the post office to mail the announcements.

His timing was perfect but subconscious. All afternoon, he never once thought that track practice would be over at 4:15 nor that Coach Rose would go to the post office on his way home. He never actually thought about it, but he knew it. So he was not surprised when the two met at the stamp-licking table.

Coach Rose's habits were infrequently discussed but well known about the community. He was a young man when he first came to Wheatheart, but he had brought with him the middle-age sternness it took to win the state championship his second year of coaching, and he never seemed young again. All the teachers had first names when they went downtown, everyone except Miss Bell who had taught first grade for thirty-one years, and Coach Rose. Coach Rose was the most popular man in Wheatheart, but he had no real friends. Perhaps that was the price of reverence. Football coaches, at least those as good as Coach Rose, must maintain an aloofness. They must go to a closet to do their thinking, lest the community help them think. The king must reign, and the subjects must accept and support. Coach Rose's closet thinking had produced nine state championships in fifteen years and legendary loyalty. But he had no close friends. Closets are always stuffy and sometimes people assume the image of their habitat.

The coach did allow himself one close acquaintance, Mr. Benalli, the basketball coach and English teacher. The two of them ate lunch together and hung around in the halls at school, but no one understood why.

Benalli was a good coach all right; he knew his stuff and he worked hard, both in basketball and in English, but no one cared much. Wheatheart was a football town, and the football coach would have been someone special, even if he hadn't been Coach Rose.

Benalli worked hard at trying to achieve the same special image, but Rose didn't have to work at it. It all came natural to him. He was the football coach, *their* football coach; and that job gave him the mystery and the air to be a hero.

To everyone in Wheatheart, young and old alike, he was Coach Rose. Although he signed his checks A.G. Rose, no one knew what the A.G. stood for, and very few dared guess.

When Abe was a senior, the coach missed two days of practice because his mother died. Abe couldn't tell whether the team was more hurt because the coach missed practice or because they had to accept the fact that he had a mother. That was the only unexpected thing the coach had ever done, so Abe was subconsciously prepared for the conversation at the post office.

Abe felt like a glass of seltzer. "Hi, Coach." He had never been that bubbly before. He had never spoken to the coach first.

"Hi, Abe. Congratulations on your new son." The coach knew the community, but Abe was still a bit surprised.

"Thanks, Coach. Can't tell much about him yet, but he seems like a good boy."

"I saw him last night, Abe." The coach also got around a lot. "He looked fine and healthy. I am sorry about the blood change thing, but it looks like he is getting along all right now." This cut through the superficiality of the day. Abe had comfortably pushed yesterday's events over the threshold, and the town had chosen to leave them there.

"Doc says it will be all right."

"How is Mary Ruth? I didn't go in to disturb her, since she was sleeping when I was there." Coach always asked about Mary Ruth, which surprised Abe, since Mary Ruth had never been a cheerleader or anything like that.

"She's fine." Abe wanted to say more, but a coach-player relationship is a delicate one with places appropriately assigned.

"Abe, I watched Jimmy Charles a long time last night. I enjoy watching a new life and thinking of the promise it offers. Abe, be proud. You deserve to be. But also be humble. That is a precious thing you have there. New life. Learn to appreciate it." That wasn't a bad sermon from a football coach and shop teacher.

"Coach, I want him to be a good boy."

Coach Rose was still sermonizing. "Show him how, Abe. I know you will. Don't push him. Show him. He'll turn out all right."

"Coach, I want him to play. I want him to play for you."

The coach's chuckle was on the surface one of amusement but it had harsher undertones. "Want happiness for him, Abe? Don't worry about specifics like football."

Apparently the coach didn't understand, so Abe persisted.

"Coach, playing football for you is happiness. I have already bought him a ball."

Almost wearily, "If that's what he wants, Abe."

"Coach, I am going to teach him to run and to pass." Abe wanted it understood that he wasn't thinking in terms of another pulling guard.

The coach was undaunted, almost oblivious, "But Abe, let him be what he is. You are a good man. Raise a good son. I'll be proud of you for that. Football is only a tool, Abe. There are a lot more important things."

Abe was stunned. Was the coach just preparing him for more frustration, for another lifetime as a pulling guard? He thought he ought to have the final word, but he was too stunned to think of it, so he mailed the letters and started out.

Coach Rose recognized his discomfort and made one last verbal gesture. "I am looking forward to getting to know your son, Abe. I hope he is half the man his father is."

Abe slowed his steps and would have spoken, but tears blocked his throat and hung there for the next sixteen years.

Three days later, Abe brought his son and Mary Ruth home. He acclimated rather well to the events of the evening—the feeding, the burping, bathing the soft skin, and the potential. Abe's bustling about was unusual; and if asked, he would have attributed it to Mary Ruth's delicate condition. But deep inside he enjoyed fatherhood. This was all new for him. Usually he disliked new things, but this was a new that was supposed to be. It wasn't contrived and forced like the transients who tried to fight their way into Main Street. This was something new which belonged, and had always belonged.

That night, Abe and Mary Ruth lay in bed awake for a long time, straining to hear sounds from the next room.

"Abe, do you like him?"

"Yeah. He's everything I thought he would be."

"He's so good. The nurses said he never cried in the hospital. And he never cried when he was with me."

"Did you get to spend a lot of time with him?"

"Yes. They brought him for me to feed him, and they left him there each time for a while."

"Did Doc ever come back to talk to you?"

"Abe, he assured me that everything is going to be all right. He said Jimmy Charles is healthy as a lark."

Abe smiled. He didn't know what a lark was and he doubted that Doc did.

"Who do you think he looks like, Mary Ruth?" That was a dumb question, but he thought she might be interested in it.

"I don't know. He's dark like all my brothers, but he's got your nose and forehead." That pleased Abe, although he suspected that she just made it up.

"Coach asked about you."

"Oh, where did you see Coach?"

"At the post office. He said there were a lot of things more important than football."

Mary Ruth spoke as if she were speaking of a father. "The coach is a wise man."

"You know what he said?"

"No," she pleaded.

"Well, he said. . . . well, he said some nice things." Abe just couldn't recite the words, not just then.

"You deserve them, Abe." Mary Ruth often understood without words. "Abe?"

"Yeah?"

"Do you think we have a good marriage?"

He hated those questions. She probably picked it up from one of those magazines in the hospital. "Sure. I am happy with it."

"So am I. And I am so glad that we have Jimmy Charles. Abe, we will be good to him, won't we?"

"The coach said he hoped he would be half the man I am." Abe blurted it out as if it were a surprise death sentence.

Mary Ruth was silent for a long time. Then she repeated, "Coach is a wise man."

There was another long silence which Abe spent wondering what she was thinking of. Finally, she broke the suspense with a seemingly mundane question which became more important than it should have been. "What kind of man do you want him to be, Abe?"

"Happy, I guess." He had no idea what that meant, but he had to stall for time.

"Abe, what if he didn't grow up to want to live in Wheatheart?" She was serious.

"What?"

"When I look at him, he is so good and so gentle and I know this is mother talk, but he looks so intelligent. Suppose he wants to be something, well—something he can't be in Wheatheart?"

It was a new thought for Abe, and he wasn't too pleased with it. "Like what?"

"Well, a doctor or a lawyer or something like that. Abe, we have to want something noble for him. Something important."

Abe matched that against all of his hours and long furrows of dreams and anticipations, and he saw no real conflict. "Yeah, I suppose you are right. We have got to want what is best for him." Abe caught a twinge of the pulling guard memory from the John Deere conversation.

"Abe, let's start as soon as he is old enough to understand and let's prepare him. I just think of how many kids we know who could have been something special in life, but they never got up enough courage to leave Wheatheart. I don't mean force him, but just make sure he knows that there are good people and happy people in other places too—that you can be happy somewhere else."

"What do we do?"

"I don't know. Travel some, I guess. We really do need to take a trip once in a while. And read to him. And take him over to the college to plays and concerts and things like that."

At the conclusion of that demand-like statement, Abe spent some moments remembering how rapidly the community had changed, and it distressed him. But he recognized this was progress, and one side of him agreed with Mary Ruth. "Sure, we will go. Just so long that we are home on the nights of the football games."

She couldn't see the seriousness of his face so she chose to make light of the idea. She giggled a flirty giggle, punched him gently in the ribs with her elbow, and teased him. "Oh, you football heroes are all alike. You think you win the girls' hearts with your muscles."

Very briefly, he wondered if she even knew that her own husband had been a pulling guard. But he couldn't let himself think that, not from his own wife. So he rolled over and slept soundly without significant dreams until the rooster crowing waked his son at 5:30 the next morning.

Gentle Rain of Promise
1966

Before Mary Ruth baked Jimmy Charles' first birthday cake and decorated it with one memorable candle, a lot of gentle rain fell into Abe Ericson's life. The dust of beginnings and struggles had settled into a prosperous but sometimes reckless maturity. Change was not entirely new to Abe. He had leaped before—in junior high school when he started playing football, when he graduated from high school, when he and Mary Ruth were married. But those were leaps. One moment he was Abe Ericson of future remembering; the next moment he was Abe Ericson, feat accomplished. Their wedding was typical of this. Abe had spent some time remembering what it would be like to be married, and he thought he had prepared himself. Nevertheless, when Brother Bob pronounced them man and wife with all of Wheatheart at the Baptist Church looking on to make it an official community action, he leaped and some of that leap ended in the unknown.

Being a father was different. He leaped every day, and every one of these leaps was into an unknown, because his prior remembering of having a son had never covered infancy. Since he didn't know what to expect from each new day, he trusted God and Mary Ruth to get him through the next leap. All those leaps added together turned Abe into a man.

He still invested some of his tractor-driving hours in future remembering of Jimmy Charles' football career, but he never quite lost the conscious reality of the present presence. As soon as it was possible and before it was safe, Abe and Jimmy Charles became inseparable. With only minor adjustments, Abe fashioned the infant seat to the pickup. Jimmy Charles learned to crawl in the kitchen, but he perfected the craft in Abe's workshop. Mary Ruth chided both of them for the red dirt and oil stains which soiled the pant knees and tender hands; but in his bosom, Abe smiled and felt noble and gallant. Those were the stains of fatherhood and they were wholesome. Jimmy Charles met the community before he walked, cradled in his father's arms. He didn't command much attention on Abe's side of the world because masculinity doesn't recognize babies—that's for women at the grocery store—but at least everyone knew that Abe had a son.

That year, a jubilant, almost festive attitude pervaded Wheatheart. The rains continued to fall, gently and well-scheduled. The young wheat plants grew into big plants. Their tops waving in the late spring wind, like magic, turned into heads of grain, with fifty, sixty, even seventy-five kernels, plump and succulent. Despite low prices, a good harvest is an unequaled joy. The grass grew. Cattle ambled contentedly from blade to blade and pond to pond. After harvest, the soil plowed up in fine texture like it used to look in the old days, not in hard dry chunks of the recent past. Without the dusty density, the winds were refreshing and pleasant. The water table raised, and watching the TV weatherman at ten o'clock each evening was no longer a dreaded chore. In fact, the year was so prosperous that some of the more religious farmers went to bed even before the news came on.

The bedtime conversations became a nightly occurrence for Abe and Mary Ruth. These were happy times of stories, observations, and predictions. Occasionally they were serious times, with exchanges of goals and aspirations.

A few weeks after Jimmy Charles had come to adorn the Ericson household, the conversation one night took a bizarre cast, and events produced by their talk brought Abe pain and joy for years.

Mary Ruth initiated most of the conversation. With a mother's instinct, she lay awake assessing the sounds of silence emanating in the other room; and she solicited company in her vigilance.

"Abe, what do you think of Jimmy Charles now?"

"I guess we ought to keep him."

"Oh, Abe, be serious."

"I am serious. What kind of question is that anyhow?" He wasn't chagrined. He knew why she asked the question, and he was glad for the remembering that flowed in its wake.

"Don't you think he is bright for his age?" Other mothers would have asked that question without a reason, but not Mary Ruth. Life and appraisal were more objective for her. The question was genuine, and she had data to support the claim.

Abe had no such data. Jimmy Charles was the first baby he had ever really looked at or had studied closely. That fact had occurred to him one day as he was driving his tractor. So his question was mostly at the fact-finding level: "Why do you say that?"

"Abe, I really believe that child knows me, and you." He was pleased to be included, even if it was an afterthought. "Day before yesterday, we passed him around at Circle, and I really think he smiled when he got back to me." Circle, a church function where the women meet to talk of missionaries and coffee cake recipes, was the one luxury Mary Ruth allowed herself.

"What age do babies begin to recognize people?" Abe had never thought about it.

"Well, not this young. He just has a lot of personality. Everybody at Circle talked about it. And he never cries. He is such a happy baby."

"Is it all right if I am proud of him, then?" Abe didn't want to change the tone of the conversation that much, but he knew that

Mary Ruth couldn't answer his burning questions about the future—that would take a coach; and just then he really didn't want her to know that he had such thoughts.

"Sure. He's yours." She condescended only a bit to make that allowance. She played the ensuing silence until it ripened and plucked it at its plumpest moment. "Abe, if he is so special, maybe we ought to do something special for him."

"Such as?" He was more interested than it sounded.

"Well, I was thinking we ought to present him to the church."

"I agree. We'll take him and we'll keep him with us. I don't want any kid of mine in that nursery. He'll just go to church like everybody else."

She played the silence again, this time not quite so long. "That's not exactly what I had in mind."

"Oh?" a bit suspiciously.

"Do you remember when Lisa Ann Foster's little sister was born?"

"We were in high school, weren't we?" Abe was growing cautious.

"Yes. I went to the Methodist Church one Sunday with Lisa Ann, and they baptized her."

The Methodists do that." Abe was recalling his theological education.

"But, Abe, it was such a beautiful thing. The preacher held that little baby, and he said some nice things about her and to the parents. I have often thought I might just be a Methodist so my babies could be baptized." That wasn't entirely true. She would never be a Methodist. Abe knew that, but he still didn't know where she was going.

"Well, Baptists don't do that kind of thing, Mary Ruth." He was just reminding her.

"I know they don't baptize babies, but what about dedication or something like that?"

"I've never seen that, either."

She waited until silence had stilled the defense. "Pat Johnson told me that her cousin goes to the Baptist Church in Kingfisher, and they did that once over there. The parents brought the baby to the front of the church, and the preacher dedicated it and the parents."

"What happened?" Abe startled himself with the question. He didn't know why he was still pursuing this.

"I guess they just took it home and raised it. But Abe, Jimmy Charles is special, and I would like to offer him as something special."

"That's not mother talk, is it?" Abe was teasing her, but he knew she had a point.

"I suppose it is, but I just thought it would be something nice to do." She had virtually surrendered.

Abe waited for the idea to dissolve and drift away into the realm of absurdity, but it was too persistent. He could have thrown out the idea without too much trouble, but the images it conjured drew pangs of pleasantness. He would like that, holding his son before the church so that the world could know that this was new life and a life of hope. Then, like the chance meeting of a schoolmate who had left Wheatheart and your consciousness during the seventh grade, Abe had another thought. He remembered that dusty morning when he knelt in the soil of the Cole place and solicited the help of God. And he remembered that he had remembered to give thanks that night as he walked out of the hospital.

He broke the darkness. Hoping she was still awake, he spoke softly. "Let's do it."

"What?" She was more sleepy than dumbfounded.

"Let's do it."

"It was just a silly notion. A silly girl dream I once had. It isn't important. Like you said, Baptists don't do such things."

By this time, he had even convinced himself. "Nope. I think it is a good idea. Jimmy Charles is special, and we need to show everybody." As soon as he finished that statement, he couldn't understand why he had thought it. It was not in his character to do the unusual, to go against the standard. Mary Ruth had not been all that persuasive, either. There must be something else prompting the urge. He couldn't locate it. He had never remembered it at moments before; he had never thought about it. He hadn't made plans or provisions, but he knew that he liked the idea.

In an almost triumphant tone he pronounced the conclusion. "We'll do it. We'll invite Brother Bob out for supper and just tell him what we want to do. He'll know how." And with that simple strategy, the revolution was planned.

Brother Bob came for supper. While his wife helped Mary Ruth by holding the baby, Brother Bob followed Abe through the evening chore routine, looking rather awkward in his white short-sleeved shirt and preacher fat. Several men in Wheatheart had enlarged stomachs from diets of excessive starches, but Brother Bob was getting flabby all over. He wasn't that way when he first came to Wheatheart, fresh out of Bible college. Abe was in high school then, but the preacher could hold his own in touch football games and backyard basketball. But too many meals cooked special by ladies who were trying to impress the young preacher had widened his middle, slowed his reflexes, and softened his muscles.

Although he was not a native, Brother Bob adapted to Wheatheart life. He had been raised somewhere down in the cotton country in the southern part of the state and had known the thrill of poverty and hard work.

His coming to Wheatheart was accidental, but his staying was with purpose. When the old preacher retired, the pulpit committee looked all over the state for a replacement, but couldn't find the right man. When Brother Bob came one Sunday to preach just for the day, the search terminated. No one could quite identify the magic of the relationship. His accent was a little more Southern, his vowels more rounded, and his Bible red. Some thought that he reminded them of Billy Graham.

Brother Bob wore the power of popularity gently. He was persuasive in the pulpit and out, but he was never pushy. He was a denominational man, a bit too much so, Abe sometimes thought.

But somehow he presented the denominational projects in such a way that the people thought they at least had a choice. Everyone knew that Brother Bob was a young riser in the denomination, but he had been in Wheatheart for nine years. In that time he had almost become a native.

After the chores, the supper, and the necessary talk, they got down to business. Over the years, Brother Bob had perfected the technique of diplomatic abruptness which is necessary in the reportoire of a busy man. "Now what is this I hear you want to do?"

Abe wanted to stare at Mary Ruth and keep silent, but that wouldn't have been manly. The one thing he wanted the preacher to know was that he was the master of his own house. "Well, we want to dedicate Jimmy Charles."

Each stole a casual glance at the baby who was by now asleep in the arms of the preacher's wife.

Brother Bob spoke as one with infinite but studied wisdom. "Well now, I don't need to tell you good people that the Baptists don't baptize babies."

Abe interrupted. "We don't mean baptize. We just want to dedicate him."

"The Scripture is plain about this, Abe. A person is not to be baptized until he is old enough to decide for himself. Christ didn't baptize babies. A person must choose to be a Christian; then we baptize him into church membership."

Abe repeated himself. He didn't know why Brother Bob hadn't heard the first time. "We don't mean to baptize him. Just dedicate him." He made it very plain.

Brother Bob used time to marshal defense and then relinquished. "Well, I guess we might be able to do that. As long as you understand that this doesn't really mean anything. He will still have to be saved, just like everyone else. And be baptized when the time comes."

Mary Ruth came to Abe's rescue. "We know that."

Seeing that he couldn't escape, Brother Bob started an end-around move. "I guess we could do something special. I'll call a couple of friends of mine, men who have been in the ministry longer than I have, and see if there is a service for this. I can't get ready this Sunday, but we can do it a week from now, if you still want to then."

Mary Ruth was calm when she spoke, but Abe found her speech reassuring. "We will still want to." And the movement took shape.

Brother Bob brought simplicity into the service, simplicity engineered to minimize emphasis and endorsement, but which in reality created a rural and raw beauty. Just after the offering, he stepped to the front of the podium and asked Abe and Mary Ruth to meet him there. They came, with Abe carrying their posterity and Mary Ruth beaming her pride. A hush unusual for a Baptist service fell on the congregation, and Abe tried to decide whether it was reverence or shock. Brother Bob held Jimmy Charles so the congregation could see and explained that dedication was allowable in Baptist circles. With reference to Samuel of the Old Testament, he said something about parents offering their children to the service of God, and reminded Abe and Mary Ruth and all parents present of the awesome responsibility of childrearing. After offering a short prayer which flowed more smoothly than his usual pulpit prayers, Brother Bob notified the congregation that the parents and child would be at the front of the church when the service was over, and that the congregation should come forward and offer "the right hand of fellowship to these young parents." With that, the three returned to the pew, Brother Bob hastened to his sermon; and Abe fidgeted through the rest of the service.

Following the benediction, they took their place at the front. The people made a circle around the church and came by orderly. Those who came offered congratulations and best wishes, and most were genuine. Abe noted those that avoided the line; he noted those who were embarassed, reticent, and even rude. He noted and pondered these events and concluded that he had made the right mistake.

Remembering the Future
1966-1970

Jimmy Charles adorned childhood. He used it to model grace, wit, innocence, curiosity, and sensitivity. For most of childhood, he brought fleshly credence to baby food commercials. He participated in the usual calamities, measles, high fever, mumps, bumps and bruises. He went through the appropriate stages, the first tooth, the first step, the first word, the first sentence and the first cute imitation of adulthood. He went through those stages in the appropriate sequence, but always a few weeks or a few months ahead of the schedule. Mary Ruth never consulted Dr. Spock; she didn't need to. She had a mother and a mother-in-law to keep her current of all the methods, tried and new. But she knew that Jimmy Charles was ahead of schedule, and she reported regularly to Abe as they summarized their days and lives in their bedtime conversations. Abe had reports of his own for those occasions; but despite the pride and the hyperbole, neither ever quite revealed the depth of their own perceptions.

As Jimmy Charles developed in speech and movement, the John Deere store became an even greater scene of pleasure and frustration for Abe. It wouldn't have been appropriate for those scions of agribusiness and loafing who decorated the place to have remembered a child's name, so Jimmy Charles was christened "Little Abe." Abe was proud of the title, but only on the surface and in the present. He still had plans for the future; and in the future, they would remember his name.

Abe and Little Abe went into the store often for such things as a new set of plowshares. In the past, Abe would have taken the old set to the blacksmith shop to have them whetted to a fine point again, but since the rains had begun to fall, he didn't have to grind old metal until it became sharp. He could buy new.

The Garlands were just as friendly as they had been during the droughts and winds, but with more purpose. The crowds weren't as large, either, and that probably pleased the proprietors in a subtle way. Farmers farmed more in times of prosperity and moisture, and just didn't have as much loafing time. Instead, they stayed out in the fields until the seedbeds had been worked free of clods and into fine red powder. With skills that had lain dormant in more depressing times, they plowed in old furrows and ditches and created new water routes for the now plentiful flow to run smoothly into the canyons and creeks without cutting deeper furrows through now valuable soil. When the fields had been tilled to perfection, the farmers with a sense of beauty and order cut weeds around the fence rows repaired machinery and buildings. They came to the conversation spots only to buy and to catch abbreviated news updates. Since they didn't linger as much, the conversation was short, fresh, and complete. Usually, the stories were new.

Despite the season and the rush, Abe was never too busy to be friendly nor to add to his remembering deposit, so he stopped at the corner of the half-walled squares which suggested offices and served as reference points for community meetings. Jimmy Charles went directly to the open boxes of hardware at the end of the counter and started assembling the nuts onto the bolts with the intensity of a Nobel experimenter. Others gathered around, plus whichever Garland happened to be there, and took turns at reporting, commenting, and remembering.

Charlie Brady was in the middle of a depression story with old data and new details. "I think he died in the spring of '32." Art Garland verified the story and the date with a nod of his head. "Everybody around here loved Clint Emerson, everybody. He had a lot of kids and they all worked hard. Times were bad, but he had so many friends and relations that we knew there would be a big bunch. People would come if they could."

Some philosopher interrupted. "Yeah, that's the way to have a big funeral, die in your prime."

Charlie won the floor back with a quick dash at the period. "Sure. Well, we knew there would be a lot of people there, and we had to feed them something. I only had about twenty old hens and everyone of them was a layer—a good layer—eggs every day. But I said to the old lady, 'Man's got to do what a man's got to do' and we killed one of those good layers. Like killing one of my own kids, I tell you. Taking food right out of your mouth. But we killed her and took chicken and dumplings. Always had plenty of flour so we had dumplings." With that Charlie concluded the depression admonition and settled back to wait for young people to grasp the meaning of their fortunes.

From there the conversation darted and skirted through rain measurements, wheat prices, new tractors, cattle prices, local deaths, and land transactions; but eventually and always, they got to football.

Scott Garland started it by remembering something significant from the near past. "You know who was in the store the other day?" Rather than a question, that was designed as a transition to get the conversation onto a new form. He answered himself. "Carl Williams."

The name invoked a reverent, silent, nonvisible gasp from all the participants. Abe, himself, felt a slight blush and hoped that it wasn't conspicuous. Carl Williams had been the first and probably the greatest, if not in reality, at least in legend, of Wheatheart's modern all-state backs. It was he who had carried the Whippets through the undefeated state championship season of 1952. When

Abe was a small boy and had first played football on the wonderful fields of his imagination, he had been number 24, Carl Williams. In that world, Abe in Carl Williams' body had run with abandon, had roamed the streets with acclaim, and had courted the cheerleaders with dexterity. Abe first tasted the success of Wheatheart football through Carl Williams' fame.

After high school, Carl had gone to the University and had played there enough to letter. Now he was a lawyer somewhere near Oklahoma City and visited the home folks just often enough to keep the legend alive. Whatever he might be where he lived now, he was a hero at home, handsome and mysterious. He visited all the old places but talked very little. When people recalled his heroics for him, the touchdowns and the victories, he listened expressionless and without comment; and it seemed that the yardage got longer and the would-be tacklers got bigger each time he came home.

Someone started the "Let's remember" process with a comparison. "You know, I was thinking of Carl the other day. That young Jessup kid reminds me of him, some. The way he runs with his toes pointed out."

A legend protector hastened a protest. "Yeah, but he will never be as fast. Carl had speed. Speed out of the stance, and he accelerated." Abe appreciated that comment, which spurred his remembering.

The comparer relinquished just a bit. "I know that, but he is young and he does turn his toes out real funny." Paper records, those kept in dusty files in the back room of the coach's office, would have, in fact, revealed that the Jessup boy was faster than Carl had been at this stage in development; but no one looked because mental records were truer.

And the mental records were lifted out of the files as the conversation grabbed at heroes from both Wheatheart and enemy schools, past and far past, and glorified them in legend.

Abe participated with a silent smugness, content to wait, to wait as long as it took, for he knew that someday his role in this circled conversation would be more important than that of a pulling guard.

While most minds and tongues pointed to the past, Abe's mind flickered sneak previews into a more rewarding future. And just as he was about to be seized by and released to an embodiment of those dreams, a small hand tugged at the hammer holder on the legs of his overalls, and a small voice pleaded, "Daddy, let's go home."

Most men cherish obligations of production but still complain about them. Abe didn't complain. Tractor-driving became even more fulfilling than it had been before. Now he had company. Now he had a partner. Now he had an alter ego. Jimmy Charles went along every day.

As soon as his small legs grew long enough to hold the pant cuffs off the ground, he became useful. Abe called him his Johnny Boy. He wasn't sure what that meant, but he had heard someone use it once. Charlie Brady called him a gopher. Once at the John Deere place, Charlie had recognized their presence with, "Well, here comes Abe and his gopher." Actually, Abe would have liked that even better than Johnny Boy, except that Charlie Brady had said it.

Jimmy Charles was more willing than sturdy. Abe would shout with a tone that combined demand with chuckle, "Hey, Johnny Boy! What about a 13/16 end wrench here, and be quick about it." The small legs would pedal through the dirt to the tool box, the small hands would struggle with the heavy box lid, and the untrained mind would guess at what that strange word, 13/16, must mean. Between them they perfected the hold-up-and-call system. Jimmy Charles would hold up a wrench and ask, "This one?"

"Nope."

"This one?"

"Nope."

"This one?"

"Yep, that's it. Bring it over here."

So, the wrench was produced; the plow was repaired; and both men, father and son, beamed their satisfaction. Abe had done more work and was not as tired at day's end. He noticed that, but he did not notice that Jimmy Charles knew which was the 13/16 wrench the next time it was needed. Mary Ruth would have noticed, and would have commented; but Abe didn't, not now, at least.

For the wheat farmer, fall is the season of faith. He spends his days and evenings, energy and Diesel, preparing the red dirt altar. He drags many toothed implements across long fields until he has broken the clods, induced the moisture to the top, mixed the sand and the loam into a sifting texture, and has brought the clean smell of fertility to the countryside. Then, when the rich red dirt is fine enough to present to the Master, the farmer, in bewilderment and worship, thrusts in his frail, precious seed. Despite all the television farm programs he has heard and all the USDA pamphlets he has read, he still doesn't understand the process. He knows what takes place scientifically, but he doesn't know why. Science may be able to put men on moons, but putting seed in soil is still an awesome, holy experience. Wheat plants are too fragile and there are too many enemies—greenbugs and grasshoppers, late freezes and fire, floods, blight, smut, weeds, and the ever-threatening drought.

But in wheat country, God recognizes the faith demanded in the fall. He puts an aroma of promise, of freshness, of fertility into the soil and into the world. He spangles the sky with stars so rich and clear that even good farmers, who don't have to, frequently stay in the fields past dark just to be a part of the beauty of the night. He gives them brisk air, not abrupt but brisk. He gives them stillness so that diesel smells and engine purrs are sharper, more rewarding during the wheat-sowing process. He paints the world with cool redness so that men are happy to be a part of it. And He gives them football.

Abe was always very spiritual in the fall, and Jimmy Charles, even before his fourth birthday, had become a vital part of this.

To save labor, Abe employed a dual process. He pulled the drill behind the clod-cutting tandem disc and combined those two operations. It was slower that way, and it took more tractor power; but Abe had figured it out, never on paper but many times in his remembering moments; and he had concluded that this was the most efficient method. Thus, this procedure became a part of his identity. If a transient had asked a native for a description of Abe Ericson, this system of wheat-sowing would have been mentioned early in the account.

Although Mary Ruth worried, Jimmy Charles was perfectly safe riding on the tractor all day. With mostly hidden reluctance, she gave in, demanding only time for the daily naps. But after that, she would interrupt her own schedule to return Jimmy Charles to the field, so that the two men in her life could finish the day together. After all, Abe knew what he was doing. He was a master tractor driver, and careful. And Jimmy Charles was so excited about riding with his father.

As Abe directed his machinery through the preparing and planting operation, Jimmy Charles sat on a specially mounted toolbox which gave him a wide perspective. Yet, he spent most of his time looking backward. There was something about the tumbling dirt swishing against the scoured-clean metal that fascinated him. By the hour, he sat quietly and watched, while his father produced and remembered the future with a fleshly certainty at his leg.

Just as the last tip of the sun fell below the flat horizon and the sharp red of sunset jumped up to meet the deep blue of the clear fall night, Abe realized that the lengthening shadows would soon limit Jimmy Charles' dirt watching. Abe did not actually consciously analyze that sunset scene as an artist might have. He didn't have to look at or account for it. He knew it was there, and he was fully appreciative of its beauty, but he saw it differently than an artist would. He was a native and was part of it. It was part of him. That sunset was beautiful beyond measure, prettier than any building or any garden or any fountain or any picture that man had ever made. But it wasn't worth getting excited about. It just meant that dusk, darkness, and stars would follow soon.

"You like the dirt, Son?" Short sentences and few syllables were wise utterances on moving tractors.

"Where are the weeds?" Jimmy Charles was asking from curiosity, not disappointment.

"I've killed all the weeds here. They would hurt our wheat."

"You're a good farmer, aren't you, Daddy?" Jimmy Charles might have picked that up from one of Mary Ruth's conversations with a neighbor, but Abe was wise enough not to pursue the source. He accepted it as Jimmy Charles' own.

"Tired?"

"Can I get off? I can't see."

"Sure. I'll stop here and you can go over and play by the pickup."

"Okay."

"Jimmy Charles."

"Yes?"

"Be sure and stay by the pickup so you won't get in the way of the tractor." Abe's mind flashed to all the horror stories he had ever heard about farm implements and sons, but the image was too painful and he quickly pushed it back into the subconscious.

Carefully, he pulled the rig to a stop, released the clutch and for good measure took the tractor out of gear as Jimmy Charles climbed down and rushed to the safety of the pickup. Abe's study of those stubby legs plowing through the dirt provided him impetus for the next two hours of remembering. As he worked into the darkness, he was able to focus his attention on the future. . . . The game would be, of course, the state championship game against some now unknown foe. The field would be Taft Stadium in Oklahoma City, with all the trappings and excitement of urban traffic. Or better yet, if he could dare dream of it, the field would be Owen Field at the University in Norman. Yes, it would be Owen Field. . . . As the seed trickled into the soil, Abe lived through the jars and bolts of the entire game. He did not concentrate on the pulling guards, though. In fact, he did not even see the pulling guards in his mental scheme; but he watched the backs as they slid and cut and ran for yardage, and one of those backs was Jimmy Charles. His legs were longer now, but the essence was still that of the young body which just moments before had sat on the toolbox by Abe's leg. . . . The game is close for a while, but late in the fourth quarter—no, early in the fourth quarter so some pressure can be put on the defense—Jimmy Charles takes a pitch around the right end. He comes running strong toward the sideline with some inconspicuous player blocking the pursuit from the backside. As the corner back makes his move to tackle for a loss, Jimmy Charles hip fakes him inside; then he outruns everything to the sideline stripe. For the next sixty yards, Jimmy Charles runs down that sideline through the arms of every defensive player on the field.

From his tractor seat, Abe has excellent perspective. He views that magificent run from above, behind, in front, and the side; and he experiences it. He feels the turf pass underfoot at each step, he wrenches free from each would-be tackler, he feels the wild exhilaration of pain as bodies crash against the plowing legs. And as Jimmy Charles overpowers the last man and plunges into the end zone, Abe participates in the spontaneous celebration. He pictures Jimmy Charles' calm face amidst the mass of bodies of happiness and elation, and he feels the satisfaction of having achieved greatness, of having produced in the time of crisis, of having contributed something to the legend books of Wheatheart. . . .

Suddenly Abe realized that it was dark and time to go home. He pointed his tractor toward the pickup, but drove slowly until his searching headlights distinguished Jimmy Charles playing in the dirt. There he was, kneeling in the luxury of the most beautiful playground in the world—fresh red, moist dirt. Abe remembered his own childhood.

"Whatcha doing, Jimmy Charles?"

"I'm building a town," and he kept at it.

"Oh. Whatcha call that town?" When he talked to his own son, those were not dumb questions.

"Jimmycharlestown."

"Hey, that's a good name. You'll know when you get home, that way." He didn't know what it meant either, but it seemed to make some sense to Jimmy Charles.

"Yeah. It's a good town."

Even in the dirt and in the darkness, Abe recognized the similarity between Jimmycharlestown and Wheatheart, but he decided to pursue it anyhow. "What's this big building, here?" and he pointed to a huge mound of dirt strategically placed near the edge.

"Wheat elbator."

"Oh, good idea. Farmers can get their wheat trucks there easy."

"Yeah, but trucks can come to town. I like trucks in town."

"What's this building down here?"

"John Deere store."

"Oh, hey, I should have known. What's this?" Abe wasn't just being fatherly. He was enjoying the tour.

"Pickup store."

"Pickup store?"

"Where you buy pickups, and they fix them up for you."

"Oh. What's this?"

"Store," and realizing that was not sufficient, "where the people can get food so they can be healthy."

"I'll bet this is the hospital next to it."

"Yes. I want people to be healthy."

"And what's this?"

"School, where the kids go to have a good time." Jimmy Charles might have heard that from someone else, but Abe couldn't remember when or where.

"Oh, yeah. We have to have a school. But where's the football field?"

The young architect never looked up. "We don't have a football field. The people in Jimmycharlestown all like each other."

"I swear to you, Abe, that's the smartest baby I've ever seen."

Abe didn't know; he had never been around a child before. But he was willing to accept Mary Ruth's opinion. He just wished she wouldn't call him a baby. He was nearly four years old and going on manhood any day now.

In the quiet of the night, she waited for some response, and filled that moment thinking that Abe was even more silent these days than he used to be. She decided to continue the conversation, even if she had to do it alone. "Everybody says so, Abe. The women at Circle talk all the time. Or at least, when you give me a chance to take him with me."

Abe had to defend himself. He knew she was kidding, but in a serious way. "Well, he is good help."

"That's what gets me. Abe, do you realize that kid is only three years old? Three-year-old kids shouldn't be good farmers, at least for another year or so."

He knew she was teasing him now, but he liked it. Jimmy Charles was filling the present, and with more than his presence. "He takes orders good."

"Oh, Abe, you're just being modest. That kid does everything you tell him to. He is so proud of you that it scares me, the way he tries to please you all the time."

"By then, Abe's face was red, but he knew that Mary Ruth couldn't see it. So he tried to talk without letting a lingering tear in his throat show in his speech. "Do other women ever bring their babies to Circle?" Maybe she wouldn't understand that question and answer it anyway. It was a bold risk, but he felt he had to take it.

If she understood, she didn't show it. "No, not really. None of the other women have babies that age. But I saw Sue Garland with their child in the doctor's office the other day."

Now they were getting somewhere. Abe warmed up to his pumping. After all, this was a Garland, Scott's legacy, the quarterback to be. "Oh."

"Yes. He's a little older than Jimmy Charles, but Jimmy Charles was doing a lot of things he couldn't do. You could just tell that Jimmy Charles was smarter, more alert. He carried on a conversation with everyone there and acted so grown-up."

"Was he any bigger?" That was the crucial question.

"Not that I noticed." She never had the important facts. He would have to continue to dream in a vacuum.

"Abe?"

"Yes?"

"We are so lucky. Do you realize that he has never caused us one minute's trouble?"

Abe remembered one trip to Oklahoma City in an ambulance, but he decided not to bring it up. "I guess he is pretty good."

"Too good, sometimes, I think. Too willing."

"Aren't you proud of him?"

"Frankly, it scares me."

And that frightened Abe, so he decided to ignore it. He rolled over and went to sleep.

Since high school, Abe had been a football sideline rover, one of those very dedicated fans who couldn't be confined to the bleachers but stood along the sidelines and followed the ball and the action up and down the field. No one knew how they got started. Perhaps the practice began way back before Wheatheart even had bleachers and the people had had to stand. By the time comfort came for the weaker ones, this band had become so accustomed to running the field that they couldn't be confined. When Abe was old enough to play football, they were a legend, and something of a nuisance—at least to the referees.

Coach Rose called them bird dogs. That might have offended some people, but since Coach Rose himself said it, no one acted offended.

Abe actually became a member by accident, quite unintentionally. Players seemed to look upon this group with something of a sympathetic levity. The more aggressive players, those who wore the romance of impudence around town (backs and linebackers mostly), would openly tease the bird dogs; and they were frequently the subject of postgame locker room jesting (only after the Whippets won, of course). Knowing this, Abe had promised himself never to be a sideline rover, and he meant to keep that promise. But during the first game of that first season after he graduated, he went down to the cable at halftime to chat with Roger Schmid who had played tackle beside him for two years, and Abe never went back to the stands. After they were married, Mary Ruth didn't mind. She didn't watch the game all that much anyhow. So Abe would roam the sidelines with the dedicated fans and frustrated has-beens, while Mary Ruth sat in the stands visiting with her high school friends, checking up on the gossip, and evaluating the cheerleaders and band routines.

It was a good arrangement, but Jimmy Charles changed all that. When Mary Ruth mentioned it, Abe could see her point.

"Abe, I'm afraid I'm not going to be able to manage that baby in the stands by myself."

Abe had never intended for her to. He suddenly realized that he had not covered in his remembering where Jimmy Charles would spend the games during infancy, but Abe knew that they should be together. "Okay. I'll sit in the stands and help you."

"A lot of help you'll be. But I'll take anything I can get. I would ask my mother, or your mother, but I don't think that's quite fair. After all, he is our responsibility."

The idea of having someone else participate in this crucial phase of Jimmy Charles' education shocked him. This was a father's job. "No. I'll be there."

"Well, just don't get too involved and fall off the bleachers with him."

Abe didn't mind Mary Ruth's sense of humor, except when she teased him about football. Even though she was a woman, at least she was a native, and she really should understand things better.

Abe finished the conversation silently by remembering the time just before the semifinal state game that the town had closed down at four o'clock and all the citizens—merchants, Doc Heimer, and all—marched to the field and conducted a pep assembly. The players were introduced one by one as they ran out on the field and shook hands with the coaches and Art Garland and the mayor. The story was clear in Abe's mind, and he felt his own heart beating in rhythm with the drums when he ran through the lines formed by the band. Yet, this time, the story had changed. This time, Jimmy Charles, as captain and sure-thing all-state back with great credentials, stood up and made a speech. He assured the crowd of a victory, because the team was loyal to the town. The applause was overwhelming. . . .

As it turned out, Mary Ruth probably didn't have as much to worry about as she had thought. Jimmy Charles was no problem at the games. Even as a baby in arms, he stayed awake throughout, studying the field. Coach Rose would have said that he did it with intensity. He smiled at the ooglers and googlers who came by to pester them and make over the baby; he wrinkled his mouth and shook his head when he sucked the dill pickles the FHA girls sold; but mostly he sat on his mother's knee and watched the game. When he grew past the lap stage, he simply moved his location to a place between Mary Ruth and Abe and kept up his intensity.

Mary Ruth noticed that other babies became cross during the games, particularly on cold nights when the temperature dropped to the low forties. She noticed that other toddlers were impatient. Mothers brought toys and detractors to keep them interested as long as possible. The sturdier ones roamed the stands, stepping on feet, sticking chocolaty hands on wool skirts which had to be dry cleaned, and being nuisances. Mary Ruth noticed those things, but Abe didn't. He was too involved with the ball game, the one on the field, and the one in his mind which came to the surface of consciousness during the dead spots and brought a pleasant smile to Abe's eyes.

During those dead spots, Abe would turn and look at Jimmy Charles so close beside him. Quickly, so quickly that no one ever caught him at it, he would turn and stare into the face, still intensely studying the field and players. Abe was frustrated by the distance between them. How he wanted to crawl behind those eyes to see what it was they studied. He wanted to crawl inside that mind and know what thoughts, what ambitions, what anticipations of joy and elation moved it to concentration. He was happy for the goodness Mary Ruth talked about, but it wasn't enough.

That particular night had been a good one. Wheatheart had won easily, as they usually did against Shattuck. Coach Rose had begun to put in the second string early in the second quarter, in an attempt to hold the score down; but he still coached the game with foxlike cunning, running the gap-eight defense in the middle of the field on first down, passing long on a third down and short from his own forty. These were the things which made him Coach Rose. Natives and former players appreciated these things and remembered them. Monday morning at the cafe or the John Deere store, when they evaluated the game, they would point this out with pride. Coach Rose was a humanitarian, but he was also a football genius.

Mary Ruth was happy too. The cheerleaders had some new yells; the band was in step for a change (in Wheatheart football players sometimes had to march in the band during halftime to fill up the sections, so their routines were not always as well-rehearsed as those of other bands); and one of her friends was back seeing the game. The friend's husband was an assistant coach at Apache, and they were back scouting Shattuck. In the course of the conversation between the two—girlish chatter, Abe thought—Jimmy Charles had become even better than he really was. Abe's legacy was as splendored as the October night sky above.

In the car going home, he decided to drill a hole through the joy in his throat, and let it run through his system.

"Well, Jimmy Charles, what did you think of the ball game?" That sounded fatherly enough, he thought. Mary Ruth shouldn't get suspicious.

"I liked it." His response was a little louder than normal. He might have been fighting off sleep and had turned up the volume to shock his system, or he might have been excited.

While Abe was trying to phrase his next question, Mary Ruth came to his rescue. "Well, I should say you did. You just sat there and ate two boxes of popcorn and two dill pickles." For Mary Ruth, that was what was meant by keeping statistics. This talk was all irrelevant, but it gave Abe time.

"So you liked the game?"

"Yep." To his mother, he said "Yes," but to his father he sometimes said "Yep."

"What did you like best about it?" Now he was getting somewhere. There were a lot of possibilities here, bright uniforms, exciting plays, long runs, pretty passes; but Abe was confident that the answer would be one of the right ones.

Jimmy Charles thought for a while. He screwed his little face into an inquisitive position and gave the question his serious attention. "Where the grass is green."

Abe had to rethink the night to remember what he meant, but down on the west end, opposite where the team warms up and does calisthenics, the grass is always taller and stays green longer. But tonight, that was where the Jessup boy had originated his twenty-nine yard run around the right end. Not a flashy run—particularly against Shattuck—but a fundamentally sound piece of halfback running. Abe was pleased with the answer.

"So you liked where the grass is green." Abe felt like the world's greatest psychiatrist. He had climbed inside the human brain, and had found what he had been looking and hoping for.

"Yep. That grass would make our calf fat. Wouldn't it, Daddy?"

In the stillness of the October night, there was a momentary, eternal silence, until Mary Ruth burst out laughing. She didn't say anything; it would have been easier if she had. She just laughed the laughter of motherhood. She had just gathered a precious gem to be shown promiscuously to all the busybodies in the world. That statement would make the rounds.

Abe tried to laugh too, but he couldn't. So he tried to imagine the scene—his butcher calf grazing on the football field; but there was something sacreligious about it, so he put it out of his mind.

Putting Away Childish Things
1970

The big yellow school bus rolled up to the driveway gate, and Jimmy Charles disappeared into its unknown regions. Mary Ruth observed the event from inside the screened back porch, and she remembered it and retold it with the precision of womanhood and the possessiveness of motherhood.

"You should have seen it. . . . he was so cute. He just walked out to the gate and stood and waited. He was so dressed up in his new jeans and in those silly cowboy boots Abe insisted he had to have. I will admit, though, that he looks good in them, with his stubby legs and all. Then when the bus came, he just climbed in without ever looking back. He looked like a little old man going off somewhere to do something really serious—maybe like a soldier going to war. It was just the way he climbed on that bus. . . . he put so much purpose in it."

The response of the listener was custom-courteous. "Oh, I'll bet you're really proud of him." And the more experienced or more loquacious ones would add some comparison story designed to make Jimmy Charles look good to his mother. "I remember when Joey started. He bawled everyday for six weeks and I had to go out to the bus every morning until Halloween.''

Mary Ruth's response to that kind of gesture was also custom-courteous but with a twinge of sincerity. ''Yes. I'm proud of him. But sometimes it almost scares me to see him so grown-up.''

Abe witnessed the school beginning from a point hidden away deep in the darkness of the barn. Early that morning, he had lied to Mary Ruth and to himself about the pile of chores and work he had to finish that day, and had retreated to the barn without so much as a post-breakfast conversation. He didn't understand his feelings about this event. It was almost as if Jimmy Charles were beginning a journey, and he couldn't get to where Abe wanted him to go if he didn't make that journey. But Abe was going to be impatient during the trip. While he could hardly wait until the journey was fulfilled, he didn't want it to start either.

When Jimmy Charles disappeared into that school bus, he passed into a far off world. The present was suspended by the future. Throughout the days and years to follow, Abe would accidentally catch himself wondering if Jimmy Charles even existed during those times when they were separated. What was he like? Did he talk much? What did he say? Was he popular with the other boys? Did adults like him? But Abe didn't think those thoughts long. He wouldn't let himself—they didn't seem normal.

So Abe spent his days johnny-boying for himself and remembering the future. He did spend some of his time thinking that it would be nice to have another son now, and start all over from the beginning once more. To his surprise, Abe found that he liked childhood, now that he was used to the idea, and that he would like to go through it again.

But Doc had said, ''No.'' It was too risky, for both Mary Ruth and the next baby.

''You almost got a miracle, the way it is,'' Doc had said. ''Why press your luck again?''

Abe settled for that, and went about his business during the day, knowing that Jimmy Charles would get off that bus again at 3:30 and they would be together.

At night, Mary Ruth conducted debriefing sessions with such vigor that it seemed as if she too were trying to pry into that part of Jimmy Charles' life they had been locked out of; but in reality, she was only practicing motherhood. Good mothers took an interest in their child's schooling, particularly during the early years, and they helped the teachers as much as they could. Since farm mothers didn't spend alot of time at school, they confined their supplementing efforts to nights. Mary Ruth was good at it, and Abe was excited about the possibilities—until he saw the limitations.

"Well, Jimmy Charles, what did you do in school today?"

"Oh, we read a good book. It was about a boy. He lived in town and didn't have any animals except a dog. I felt sorry for him. It doesn't seem fair for kids to have to grow up in town, does it?"

Later, Mary Ruth laughed about that when she mentioned it to Abe. "You can sure tell whose son he is, Abe Ericson. He even thinks just like you do. What have you done to my boy?" She was teasing him in her voice, but underneath the voice she was warning him too.

Abe wasn't afraid of the warning, but he was sometimes afraid the statement might not be true. One evening when Mary Ruth had wearied of her efforts to discover whether Jimmy Charles could read better than the other children in the first grade and how many addition facts each could do, Abe decided to ask some real questions.

"Son, what do you do at recess up there at school?"

"We play. Sometimes the other kids fight, but we play."

Abe remembered some of his own school days. "Oh, some of the older boys fight, do they?"

"Sometimes." Jimmy Charles wasn't all that interested in the subject, but Abe wanted to carry it a bit further. He knew when to quit with it, so it wasn't as if he were taking advantage.

"Who wins those fights?"

"Mostly the boys do." He was sincerely direct, but Abe was sure he had misunderstood the question.

"Which boys?"

"The boys."

"The boys?" Abe was beginning to get just a little impatient. He needed some real information, even if it was just a hint.

"Yes, the girls usually cry and run away."

"Oh. Then what happens?" He really didn't mean that question, but he was trying to keep the conversation going until he could think of his next line of interrogation.

"Miss Bell yells at them."

"Does she ever yell at you?" He really didn't want to ask that question either, although it seemed like a good one at the time.

"No," and he hung his voice just a bit. "She sometimes tells the boys they ought to be like me."

Abe chuckled with fatherly pride, "Why does she say that?"

"Cause I won't ever fight."

Abe suddenly realized that he was trapped here, and he resented it. For the next ten years he resented it. He was trapped between his sense of what was good and his sense of what was right. It was good that Jimmy Charles was Miss Bell's model for good. It was good that he didn't fight. Abe liked that, and he would have planned it that way, if he had even thought to remember such a thing during his long hours of remembering. But at the same time, there was a contradiction here, and Abe knew it. Good football players are tough kids. Abe recalled the list, carefully and frequently, and there were no exceptions. Every player, long past, short past, and present who made Abe's list—actually, the town's list—had been a tough kid. In the midst of their playing legends were also the legendary stories of their schoolyard fights and town mischief. But Abe's hope and legacy was praised by the teacher for being good. How can one be so proud and provoked at the same time?

At least, Mary Ruth's worries were wasted. Jimmy Charles adapted to school and studies like he adapted to life. He threw himself into schoolwork with his usual grown-up purpose and achieved success without a struggle. Learning in all its mystery came easy for him. What he heard he remembered. What he read he read quickly, and what he read quickly he remembered. He was courteous to teachers, and he obeyed the rules.

None of this was completely evident during the first grade with Miss Bell. Despite her reputation as a pedagogical genius, gained from nearly thirty years of teaching first grade at Wheatheart, Miss Bell never really allowed any child to get too far ahead of the bunch; and she rarely picked out one particular child for public praise, unless of course, it was a Garland or Wheeler or someone in that caste. Mary Ruth knew that. Abe did too, but it seemed unpatriotic to admit it, so he didn't.

But from the second grade on, Jimmy Charles was ahead, academically and intellectually. He learned to write cursive by watching his mother compose letters to her friends. One day, Grandmother discovered that Jimmy Charles could multiply. No one ever knew how or when he learned. He just knew. Soon after that discovery, the daily debriefing sessions ceased. Mary Ruth proclaimed them a waste of time. He was making progress without her help. She would leave that kind of mothering to the less fortunate, and she would spend her time cooking and cleaning for her family. But deep inside, she had other reasons. Jimmy Charles seemed embarrassed, not by the questions, but by the answers. It was a subtle thing, and only a mother would have noticed. But he seemed almost apologetic about being able to answer the questions—as if he sensed that his knowing was in some way putting his parents down, making them less of people than he wanted them to be. He didn't want to answer questions. He wanted to ask them. He wanted to stand before Abe and ask, "How much is an acre? How long before the calf is born? What does it mean if a cow's nose is dry?" It was as if Jimmy Charles wanted Abe to feel good about being Abe, and he wanted Mary Ruth to feel good about being Mary Ruth. He wanted to participate in their lives, instead of the other way around.

There was one conspicuous exception to this participation, but Jimmy Charles tried to keep it to himself. He wrote poetry. As soon as he discovered poetry during the third grade, he became a devoted writer. He had a knack for rhyme and rhythm, and he could write short poems in the spaces between chores and schoolwork. From his actions, it was evident that this was something he did for himself. He would go into his room with a distant look in his eye, and would emerge a few minutes later conversant and inquisitive. Although he never mentioned it or asked for confirmation, he had relieved himself of a poem.

When she first discovered this, Mary Ruth made a bigger deal of it than it was. She made motherly demands that he read his poems to relatives and guests. Stuttering and stammering, he would comply and turn red. But soon, the new wore off this genius so she left him alone. Abe was secretly glad. There was nothing more embarrassing than sitting in a room full of natives, or transients for that matter, and hearing your son read poetry, most of which Abe didn't understand anyhow.

School never interfered with Jimmy Charles' role on the farm. As soon as he materialized from the bus in the late afternoon, he went to work. He performed the ritual of the chores in complete obedience to the code, faithfully and promptly. When he was small and couldn't carry a full bucket, he carried half a bucket and made two trips. Although he worked quickly, he took time to be personal—to see each animal and each chicken as an individual entitled to quirks and personalities. He developed a system, and he never forgot. When he was sick and Abe substituted for him, Jimmy Charles had to tell Abe how to do things and what to watch out for. Mary Ruth just thought it was cute, but it made sense to Abe.

During the summer between first and second grade, Jimmy Charles became half a hand. Abe let him drive the tractor solo when they both could be in the field together or when Abe had to go to the house for water or fuel. Sometimes Abe would lie in the pickup and sleep some so he could work later at night. With both of them involved, the farming went smoothly, and Abe had the time and the freedom to see the future. Life was as full as he had imagined it could be.

During the summer when he was eight, Jimmy Charles became a

full hand and forever put away childish things. Mary Ruth protested some—"Letting a little boy like that drive big equipment all day. What if he got sleepy and fell off?"

Abe first tried teasing her, "You mothers are all alike. You just can't give up your babies." But he knew it was true, because his mother sometimes still treated him as a baby, and he secretly liked it. So he decided to use reason. "With all the power equipment on these tractors nowadays, he can operate it as good as any man. And frankly, he's smarter than most men. He doesn't take any chances, and he knows how I want things done." Although he didn't fully convince Mary Ruth, and she always twinged just a bit every time she saw or thought of her child astride that big machine, at least Abe convinced himself.

The two of them worked together with an uncanny precision. From the very beginning, Jimmy Charles made the turns and plowed the corners just as Abe would have done it himself. By that time, some farmers—the big spenders mostly—had begun to put CB radios in some of their equipment so the farmer could talk to the hired hand. But Abe and Jimmy Charles did not need radios for communication. Jimmy Charles understood what Abe wanted, and that was good enough. Even when the natives drove by, they couldn't tell whether it was Abe or Jimmy Charles on the tractor until they got close enough to see the size. The two were that much alike in their thinking.

Tractor-driving is a lone enterprise; for the unimaginative, it is lonely. Although neither Abe nor Jimmy Charles fell into that category, they did enjoy good conversation during the down times together. As they worked alongside each other to repair the break or adjust the implement, they would talk. Jimmy Charles talked about the present; Abe talked about the past and thought about the future.

"Daddy, there's a big rock over on the back side of that hill. I tried to haul it out, but I couldn't lift it," Jimmy Charles would report.

"I know. I guess it has been there for a long time, but it was just uncovered a few years ago during those dust storms." Abe knew that the last of the dust storms had occurred before Jimmy Charles was born more than eight years ago, but rural life keeps its own calendar.

"Could we haul it out with the pickup?" The young are always ambitious.

"Nope. It's too heavy. Next winter we'll put the loader on the tractor and try to get it then. Be sure to remind me."

Abe thought about where the conversation was—looking into the future, expecting something of Jimmy Charles at a future date. At this point, it was only a gesture, a dip into the great vat of expectations and plans, but it was a start. And Jimmy Charles seemed to be excited about it. Abe surveyed the possibility of pushing the start to a conclusion, to get beneath talk of wheat fields and boulders to life itself, of things to come and things to be.

"Jimmy Charles."

"Yes?" There was something about the boy's eagerness that startled Abe, that made the endeavor too risky. This was not the time for that father-son conversation.

Abe retreated, "Don't forget to remind me next winter."

Jimmy Charles was both reassuring and a bit impatient. "Okay, Dad, I won't," and with that he went back to being a man.

Jimmy Charles' reputation as a farmhand made the rounds and eventually came back to Abe in a John Deere conversation. It was just before harvest during Jimmy Charles' tenth year. By then, he had been a man for nearly two years. Abe had gone in to buy some last-minute repairs for his combine, and since Jimmy Charles was at home planting the last of the maize, Abe felt he could spare a few minutes for the conversation and some private dreams.

John Deere conversations were always topical and traditional. Transients might have difficulty staying with the flow, but the natives didn't. Intermingled with the drunk steer stories, reports of farm sales, wheat prices, and weather predictions were such topics as crime in the cities, the new President, long-haired hippies, and marijuana. But all these varieties, old and new, were always woven together with the everpresent thread of football.

Charlie Brady had not mellowed with age. "I'll tell you fellars, that marijuana is going to be the death of this nation. It's going to ruin their minds. That's dangerous stuff. They ought to lock'em all up and throw away the key. Get 'em off the streets so decent people can live normal."

Someone chided him. "Now come on, Charlie. Is that any worse than that moonshine liquor you used to make?" The town had snickered about Charlie's still for years, but only in recent and more permissive times had people dared bring it into the open.

"Nope, I ain't denying nothing. I used to make it. Supplied a lot of sick people around here during the depression. But that stuff won't hurt you, just get you drunk. Now that marijuana will kill you, boys. Maybe we ought to get back to moonshine again. Lot safer."

Someone supported him, "At least you moonshine drinkers didn't have to tie your hair up in pigtails the way these dopers do."

With that, everybody took a turn telling about some terrible account of long hair which each had witnessed first hand, or at least had known someone who had witnessed. There were stories of men who caught their hair in machines and were scalped, stories of people who had caught black widow spiders in their hair and were stung to death, testimonies of appetites being ruined in restaurants by greasy manes, stories of ponytails and curls.

Finally, Art Garland put everything into a very welcome perspective. "Well, at least that kind of thing won't ever happen in Wheatheart, not as long as Coach Rose is here. In my opinion, we have a lot to thank that man for."

In that company, that was a safe opinion.

"Sure do. Cut your hair or don't play—that's his rule." It never occurred to them that someone might not want to play.

"You've got to respect the man. He keeps our kids looking good, as well as teaching them football."

"Best looking kids of anybody we play."

As that was being confirmed around the room with nods and ughs, Abe was sharing his time between feeling glad that Coach

Rose was around to help him raise his son and dreaming of what it was going to be like to have a son on the field under Coach's jurisdiction. The game time images were so strong and satisfying that he almost didn't hear Art Garland call his name when the conversation changed.

"Speaking of good kids, Abe, I understand that boy of yours is sure making a hand." In nearly fifteen years of John Deere conversation, Abe had rarely been singled out as point-blank as that. This was a hint of the kind of thing Abe had hungered for as he had listened to those tales of completed passes and running backs. This was recognition. Now that it came, he was too confused to know what to do with it. He wanted to savor it, to hold it in his mouth and let it melt slowly; but the code demanded a modest response. Not to respond or to respond too quickly would be arrogant, and Abe wasn't arrogant. Despite all his planning, he still wasn't prepared, but he had to do the best he could. "Well, he does all right, I guess."

The people rallied.

"How old is that boy, Abe?"

"I guess he's ten." It was customary to act as if you couldn't remember your children's ages. It was also customary for the others to laugh when the father forgot, so they did.

Someone helped him out. "Sure he is. He was born right before it started raining. I remember it."

Abe was elated. Sometimes one gets so wrapped up in his own that he is surprised to discover that anyone else even notices. Obviously somebody did. The subject changed slightly.

"Well, that's pretty good. Making a hand when you're ten."

Abe wanted to tell them that Jimmy Charles had been a hand for two years, but sometimes the truth might be too much to believe. He decided not to risk it.

Charlie Brady took it upon himself not to let Abe get too puffed up. "What I want to know, Abe, is if he can run that tandem disc and wheat drill without getting it in the fence row." If Charlie Brady could farm as well as he could criticize farming, he might have made it on his own, so Abe chose not to let that ruin the moment.

But Scott Garland ruined the moment with another idea. "All that work is going to make that kid tough, Abe. He's bound to be a tough pulling guard."

Abe wanted to stop the conversation, to set the future record right, to correct the false ideas and perceptions. But as he was festering for an answer, Art Garland concluded the conversation with a dream that should have been big enough. "Abe, these John Deere people are always looking for some idea for their advertising. I think it might be kind of cute to come out and take a picture of that boy running your old combine. That might make a good pitch. Easy enough that a kid can do it. What do you think? Would you mind if I asked my block man?"

The hurt was deeper than the flatter, but Abe gathered his wits and agreed.

The company man came during harvest. It should have been a time of promise, of fall in June, a time when all of Abe's feelings for the future could take on the visible forms of actuality and present. But it wasn't, not totally, not for Abe at least. Mary Ruth had been excited and had even let Jimmy Charles wear his school clothes to work that day. But for Abe, this wasn't the moment he had dreamed about, so he held his excitement in check.

Art Garland brought the man out. Art seemed as casual and as comfortable as he would have been selling machinery back in the store, but the company man seemed impatient. He had come out here to do a job, and all other work should bow before his job. His was the important work, not the thrashing and the hauling and the plowing.

Abe thought the man might change his attitude when he discovered that a ten-year-old boy was operating the combine; but that pronouncement only made him more impatient as he studied his watch and cupped his eyes against the summer sun glare to see how far away the machine was across the field and how long it would take to be there. Finally, it did come, and the man with his high-powered camera went into action as impatiently as he had waited.

He took pictures from every angle, rushing around the moving machine, tromping down good wheat, and trying to stay clear of the whirling blades, gears, and sickles. Abe thought it was a funny scene, and he laughed about it when he remembered it in years to come—that boy-like man so serious with the business of photographing a boy commanding that machine with man-like skills. It was a game, Abe thought. The whole act of farming, the serious business of harvest itself, was just a game played by clowns with cameras and small boys who had become men before their bodies did. If farming is a game, what then is serious?

With his chronic impatience, the man decided he had to have a closer shot, so he climbed up the ladder and rode beside Jimmy Charles. Transients are capable of the unexpected, and Art and Abe both hoped he was experienced enough not to fall off and smart enough not to jump off. He didn't fall off, and he didn't jump off. He made the whole round, all the way around the big field; and when the machine came back into view, there he was, casually talking to Jimmy Charles, laughing and gesturing and taking his turn at listening. Together they made another round, and another, until it was time to dump—to auger the wheat gathered in the combine bin into the truck. As the machine stopped for that operation, the man shook hands with Jimmy Charles, backed down the ladder and wandered over to the car. There he stood, despite Art Garland's impatience to leave, and waited until Jimmy Charles again pulled the big machine into movement and disappeared into the glare of the sun. He waved one last wave, got into the car, and drove away. Abe never knew what those two, Jimmy Charles and the company man, had talked about. And he never asked, although he remembered that event, vividly, for the rest of his remembering life.

Two months later, Jimmy Charles' picture was published in the John Deere magazine, and Abe became a local hero. It was a feeling good enough in itself, but Abe could handle that good feeling in the shadow of what he expected to come.

A Roaring Silence
1974-1976

After his public initiation into the religious life on that remembered day of dedication, Jimmy Charles grew spiritually in the usual ways. He graduated from Sunday School class to Sunday School class, always with some positive comment from the teacher. At Christmas and Easter, he took his place beside the other children in front of the church and said his piece without coaching or coaxing. Each Sunday, he sat in the pew between his parents and made pictures until he learned to write and could make words.

Brother Bob was friendly enough to Jimmy Charles, with vocal jabs to show that he cared or boxing jabs to show he could even relate. But the minister never looked at him, not directly. Mary Ruth noticed it first. Then she mentioned it to Abe, and he saw for himself. At first, he thought it was just something in his imagination, and imaginations are dangerous and deceiving anyhow. But after several weeks of observation, Abe concluded that Mary Ruth was right. Brother Bob was never ever really looking at Jimmy Charles, even during the jabbing.

One Sunday, Brother Bob had finished the sermon—Abe could never remember what it was about on that day—and had started the invitation. He stepped down from the pulpit and took his "This is not Brother Bob the preacher but Brother Bob your friend and counselor" look at the front of the church.

And as if on cue, Jimmy Charles folded his writing, slipped it into his pocket, slid out of the pew, and walked up to the preacher. The two exchanged a few words; then Jimmy Charles turned and faced the congregation with an assured look.

Abe had always had some reservations about parents who rush to the front and cry over their children when they go forward, and he had remembered that he wouldn't do it when the time came. He wasn't sure why he had remembered that thing specifically. It wasn't his habit to spend his remembering time on such things. He knew that he wouldn't have anything to say and he wouldn't cry—not in church, not publicly, not so anyone could see. Besides, this was Jimmy Charles' event, and Abe was content to let him have it all by himself. He could participate from the pew.

But when the time came, Abe half wished he had not remembered so definitely. He wanted to be there. He wanted to hear the words, perhaps even to see the thoughts. He wanted to go inside Jimmy Charles' images and promises and make them his own. At least, he wanted to check on them to make sure they were orthodox. Isn't that a role of parenthood that Brother Bob talked about once?

He might have gone too—just automatically without having thought about it or remembering it—except that he felt the same urge in Mary Ruth sitting next to him, and he was awakened to his obligation to give her strength. He decided to look as unconcerned as he could, and keep his promise to his plans.

Brother Bob held up his hand and stopped the singing. He would now speak, as he frequently did in times like these; but it seemed strange to Abe that he had never really heard what the preacher said during these moments. He had heard the words before and could probably say some of them by heart, but he had never heard like he did this day.

Brother Bob began, "As we all know, this young man, Jimmy Charles Ericson, is a very special young man." Heads nodded in agreement, even some of the nervous ones. "Already in his life, he has distinguished himself." Here, the minister paused as if searching through the sermon cards for an appropriate illustration. "And as you know, he is already a national hero." Most laughed while transients and others who had not read the John Deere magazine looked at each other quizzically.

"He has come today to announce that he has surrendered his life to his Creator. He is prepared to live his life in complete obedience to the Lord's will, even by being baptized into the membership of this church; and when the time comes for his flesh and blood to be returned to the ground from whence it came, he is prepared to go forward to be reunited with his Saviour."

Throughout the church, there was a silent roar. The hush was filled with good will. Abe could sense it, but he didn't know where it came from. How was it different this time from all the other times he had watched it? These were almost the same words Brother Bob used each time, even to the "from whence it came" part where the preacher tried to sound like the Bible without really quoting. But it was different, and it was bigger than Abe. He couldn't understand it. So he just stood there and tried to look at Jimmy Charles. When he realized he couldn't do that, he entertained himself after the service by watching the crowd rush around to congratulate the preacher for Jimmy Charles' decision and by rekindling an "I told you so" spark that had lain smoldering for ten years.

When Jimmy Charles entered the fourth grade that fall, Abe went back to old duties as a sideline rover. Football watching is simply not a passive activity. The stands were all right for a while, but a man's emotions and rememberings are too big to be restricted for very long.

Now, it was even better. Jimmy Charles went with him. Jimmy Charles would crowd to the front—not an easy task among the bird dogs—and he would watch with silent intensity. Occasionally, Abe would point something out—how to take a hand off, how to lift your knees when you went through the line on the dive play, how to cut on the outside foot in the open field, how to break off the pulling guard's block. Jimmy Charles would listen, observe, and nod acknowledgment; but he never practiced. It was as if he already knew those things but didn't see any use for them. Nevertheless, the two were inseparable, on the football field as well as the wheat field. Each fall, when the wheat was sowed and the maize was cut and the play-offs over and the all-state ballots cast, Abe realized that the dreams of his remembrance were one year closer. He marked time by the falls and filled the in-betweens with the less significant details of living.

During the fall of Jimmy Charles' sixth year in school, the Whippets were good. Not only were they winning, but they were winning big. In the absence of superstars, Coach Rose and Coach Rambo had gone back to the basics—good, hard-nosed football—blocking and tackling and winning the battle of wits. That is what they were best at anyhow. There were no breakaway excitements—just long methodical drives, the kind that only natives could really appreciate, the kind that had given the community its character.

The game with Cherokee shaped up as the big one in the race for district championship. It happened that way more often than not. The two communities had a lot in common, many of the same characteristics—hearty prairie life, prosperous wheat farms, and strong-willed people. The only major difference was that Wheatheart had the legend of a Coach Rose.

The tension and ceremony began early Sunday morning, almost before the coach had had time to review the last game and relax. When the churchgoers drove up Main Street on their way to Sunday School, they passed beneath banners strung along the way. The Jaycees had been up early to notify the world—at least those people of the world who passed through Wheatheart—that history, important history, was going to occur at Whippet Stadium on Friday night. Through the week, the John Deere and Dew Drop Inn conversation was less about weather, wheat prices, and the past, and more about prophecies, predictions and hopes. And the drugstore sold stadium cushions, unusual for this late in the season. Even the transients showed some excitement.

By Friday afternoon, the passion was powerful. There was a school pep assembly in the stadium, and the band played so loudly that everyone in town could at least feel the drumbeats. The big day had come and the world should know how really big it was.

The game itself was over after the first five minutes. The Whippets came out of the dressing room filled with emotional purpose and scored on their first four possessions. After that, for the fans, it was just a matter of watching favorite individuals, remembering past achievements, and appreciating Coach Rose's chess-playing ability as he arranged bodies across the field in impregnable lines.

For Abe and the other natives, it was exciting. Natives don't need close scores and successful last-minute efforts for excitement. Excitement generates from preserving the tradition, and the more persuasive the preservation, the greater the excitement. This game would be catalogued up near the top of the memory banks and would be brought into consciousness whenever men met to ponder noble and important matters.

After the game, Abe and Jimmy Charles lingered through devotion. Although the team had long since disappeared into the dressing room to share their achievement in togethered isolation, and the custodians had turned off the north lights, Coach Rose remained in the middle of the field where he accepted congratulations, responded with embarrassed and shy kindness, looked impatient, and talked with his fans about football. Coach Rose guarded those conversations as he guarded his life. Although it seemed as if the coach were talking sincerely and profoundly, when the fan left and analyzed the conversation in retrospect, he always discovered that he had not really learned anything.

Knowing this, Abe waited casually and conspicuously at the end zone. There would be more sincerity there than in the middle of the field. In the meantime, a game developed nearby. The youngsters, grade school boys who could not yet participate in organized football, always took advantage of those moments to run and tackle in real grass, to play the game of dreams under the lights, and to imitate their heroes who had performed for real earlier in the evening. Jimmy Charles had never participated in those post-game frolics, although Abe had wanted him to. He had even mentioned it once, but indirectly. He had only said, "If you want to play with your friends out there, your mother and I would wait until you're through." Jimmy Charles had declined, of course. He never intentionally made an imposition on anybody. Abe accepted this, and told himself that it wasn't all that necessary for Jimmy Charles to mix it up with those guys. The boy was learning football standing on the sidelines, and he would get to the field when the time came. Yet, this evening Abe wished he had been more persistent. The coach was going to come by, and Jimmy Charles would be standing beside the action. Would the coach understand?

Finally, the coach did come; and although Abe was in conversation with one of the river farmers, he never lost consciousness with the moment. When he got to the end zone, Coach Rose paused and glanced at the youngsters playing on the field. His was a blank expression, one which would have been at home with a shrug. Then he turned, saw Abe, and started walking toward the gate; this time with intent and purpose.

Abe's planning was about to pay off. He was going to have the chance to introduce the coach to his son, to fill the coach's mind with the potential and the possibility, to plant a seed which was going to grow into a beautiful bloom. The timing was right; the plan was inconspicuous. All of this would seem like some significant accident. Coach Rose spoke first, "Hi, Jimmy Charles."

Abe's heart beat as if he had been wrestling steers. The coach knew Jimmy Charles. He had already seen him and could recognize him as a person, as a potential player perhaps. Abe didn't know the connection or the details, but he was happy about it.

Jimmy Charles answered, friendly but nonchalant, "Hello, Mr. Rose."

Abe wanted to scream his interruption and correction. "Coach, Jimmy Charles, Coach Rose. Never say Mr. to a man like Coach

Rose." But he chose to remain silent.

"Have you had time to read that book I lent you?" The coach was gentle.

What does he mean? What kind of book had he lent Jimmy Charles? Stories of great players? Strategy books? Maybe even the playbook—but no one gets that before his freshman year. What was going on between these two? What had happened which no one had told Abe, so he could have plugged it into his remembering moments? What had he missed that he could have already been enjoying?

"Yes, sir. I liked it. Thank you."

Is that all he could say? He liked it? Didn't it excite him? Educate him? Move him? Persuade him? Make him proud?

Jimmy Charles continued the conversation, partly because he was interested and partly because the coach was. "The Romans were interesting people. I can see why you like to read about them."

What Romans? Abe's mind retraced all his education in an instant, and pulled out of dusty drawers all he had ever heard about the Romans; but he still didn't have enough to get into the conversation. He tried to imagine Coach Rose reading books about Romans and it confused him.

But the coach answered, "I guess I like them because they were so highly organized. They knew what they wanted to do and they knew how to design ways to do it. They were the best conquerors the world has ever had because they were better organized."

It was beginning to make some sense to Abe. Football might be a lot like war. Maybe the coach did read about the Romans.

Jimmy Charles changed the tone. "I was surprised that they borrowed everything, and didn't really invent any of those things they had."

Abe was surprised too. He always thought the Romans were great inventors, when he thought about them. They built the Colosseum, he knew that, and some roads and bridges.

But Coach supported Jimmy Charles. "They are a lot like football coaches, son. We steal from anybody and everybody. The only difference is in how one coach organizes it all. There is very little originality in my life, I guess."

When you are the winningest coach in the state and have just beat Cherokee for probably the district championship, why do you need to be original? Abe had never heard the coach criticize himself, and he wished he would stop.

Jimmy Charles tried to console, "At least you didn't put the Saviour to death."

Abe didn't know where his son got that statement. It came out of his mouth, so he must have said it; but had he really thought it? Nevertheless, Abe wanted to applaud. He would have felt more comfortable if someone else had said it, but it was the right thing to say at the right time.

The coach measured his feet and the color of the grass, and answered meekly, "I would have if I had been there."

At that, Abe labeled the discussion preposterous and unreal. He would have no more to do with it. Not in the now, not in the remembering. He would treat it as if it never really happened.

The coach wasn't finished, "What did you think of that poem at the end?"

"I don't know, sir; it was too full of Latin for me to know for sure what he was trying to say."

"Yes, I suppose you're right. That's a technique some people use to make themselves seem smarter than they really are. Come by sometime and I will teach you those Latin words."

"Thank you. I would like to learn."

"I know you would, Jimmy Charles. That's why I like you. You write poetry yourself, I hear."

"Yes, sir. But just things for myself. It is something I like to do when I have some spare time."

"I would like to read some of it. If you trust me, that is, and want to show it to me."

"I would like to, Mr. Rose."

Then Coach Rose turned to Abe and said, "You have a fine son there, Abe. I am sure you and Mary Ruth are really proud of him."

Abe wanted to retreat, to retreat all the way back to player days and answer with an obedient and respectful, "Yes, sir." But he was too trapped and deserted, so he just stood there.

During the drive home, Mary Ruth and Jimmy Charles were quiet, and the stillness gave Abe the opportunity to remember the time Jimmy Charles would run eighty-five yards with a kick-off return to beat Cherokee for the district title. In-between the reruns of that beautiful picture, he tried to see if he could be comfortable remembering Jimmy Charles as a pulling guard; but the idea was foreign to him so he went back to the vividness of the touchdown run.

A Season of Promise
1977-1978

The big metal hitch which connected the back of the tandem disc to the front was bent. It was one of those mysterious bends of farming. No one ever knew when they happened or what caused them. There never seemed to be a reason—no pressure, no tension, no sharp turns. They just appeared one day. Abe had once asked the county agent about it, and he had said. "Well, metal is kind of like a man. Sometimes it just gets tired and bends or breaks. There really isn't any reason for it. The molecules in there just start jumping around and get all dislocated." That suited Abe. After all, the man had been to college to study such things.

This particular bend didn't appear to be causing any problems. The machine was operating fine. But that afternoon, the afternoon of Jimmy Charles' first day in the seventh grade, Abe decided that it needed to be fixed. So about 2:30, he lifted the disc from the ground, suspended tilling operations, and drove the rig to the barn where he could make the repairs. That is why he was convenient when Jimmy Charles got off the school bus and came ambling in from the gate.

"Hi, Dad." He sounded a little surprised.

"Hello, Jimmy Charles." He said that casually enough. "How was your first day in the seventh grade?"

"Okay, I guess. What are you doing?"

"I am fixing this bend in this hitch bar. Do you like changing classes every hour?"

"Yeah, I think it will be fun when we get used to it. I didn't know it was causing any trouble."

"It's not really, I guess, but it was bothering me." Although it might have seemed that they had formed a partnership in the farming operation, there was still a hint of feudalism; and the lord could stop and fix anything anytime it bothered him. Those were the rules. "You like all your teachers?"

"They're all nice. Did you know this tractor tire had a knot in it?"

"I saw it yesterday. I think we will drain some fluid out and try to make it get through wheat sowing. I may buy a new set this winter. Did you have football?" Abe knew the answer to that, but he had to ask. This was the day he had waited for—the first day of organized football, the day when the remembering would begin to take human form and movement. All day he had had faint visions of the now Jimmy Charles, the seventh grader, dressed up in shoulder pads—small running pads, not those big blocking pads—a slightly over-sized helmet with only one face bar, and the green jersey of Wheatheart pride. It might have been an old jersey—only a practice jersey—but it was green with the success of the legend past and future.

"Yeah. Right after lunch. This tail light has a short in it. We may have to fix it if we are going to work late this fall during sowing time." Tail lights were more necessary during fall sowing than during summer plowing.

But Abe's mind wasn't on sowing after dark or tail light shorts, but on remembering that the junior high had always practiced right after lunch, as long as he could remember. "I'll get to it sometime this week. What position did you play?"

"Left halfback. Do you think I ought to increase the calf's feed a little, now that he's getting bigger?"

Left halfback! The words pricked the reality of the present and let it ooze through all the hours and days of remembering Abe had invested in this moment. Left halfback! His dream was taking form. Left halfback! It was almost as if there were a plan—a plan that would unfold if one remembered hard and long enough. Abe's conscious turned from the blue August sky and heated sunlight to a dusty dimness of an earlier time, of the day in the hospital when Doc Heimer had told him, "You got a boy, Abe!" This was the same kind of moment. Somehow, he knew it would be a boy just as he knew it would be left halfback, but he had to wait for proof. He had faith—faith that had developed from time and energy spent on planning and remembering, but there was still a vacuum in his stomach until he heard the words for sure. Yes, Abe decided, there is a plan. In the same instant he resolved that question, he crowded in another image—of the prayer of thanks he had prayed that night in the hospital parking lot. He decided to do it again, if not the same words, at least the same thought; but he would wait until the time was riper with aloneness. Left halfback! Wheatheart was a right-handed team—that was part of the tradition; and in the offensive scheme, the left halfback carried the ball more than half the time on the dives, around end on the sweeps, off tackle on the cross-bucks. All the great ones had been leftbacks. Just as the left halfback dominated the Wheatheart game, left halfbacks, past and distant past, dominated the Dew Drop Inn and John Deere conversations. Left halfback on the seventh grade team! The plan was unfolding. From small seeds great dreams grow. Abe crowded all this into the moment and struggled against showing the fulfillment he felt. "I don't know. How much you feeding him now?"

Apparently he had succeeded. Jimmy Charles didn't detect anything; or if he did, he wasn't letting it show. "A gallon every feeding."

"Yeah. Why don't you increase it about a quarter a bucket? Be careful though. You give him too much and he will get the scours. You learn any plays?"

"No. We just ran sprints. Will we have enough seed wheat?"

"Probably not. I think I want to buy some anyway, sow some earlier variety on the Cole place. You win any?"

"I beat some, but I got beat a lot too. What kind of wheat did the Carrs have on their home place? They cut that almost a week before we started."

"Triumph. That's what I think I will try to buy. You the fastest one in the seventh grade?"

"Nope. Is the maize filling out?"

"Yeah, it looks good right now, but we will need another rain if it makes. Who's the fastest?"

"Michael Garland. Don't forget that the shaker bearing is out on the combine before we get ready to cut."

Michael Garland. The name stung, and Abe suddenly remembered why he had the vacuum in his stomach as he waited for the plan to unfold. Garland. The generation was different, but the issue was the same. That's the challenge of being a native along with all the other natives. Could it ever be different? Could the legends be rewritten? Did they have a chance even—he and Jimmy Charles? But Abe wouldn't let that ruin his moment, so he kept pounding his mind with the words, "Left halfback!" until the remembering came back into focus, and his heartbeat slowed to normal. "I ordered one last week. It will be in sometime before frost. Faster by a lot?"

"Quite a bit. You need to order diesel fuel again."

"Maybe I will have your mother call tomorrow. You second?"

"No. I used the last of the hydraulic fluid last week too."

"I'll get some more. How far back?"

"Aways. Do we need some more grease tubes?"

"There's a case in the back of the barn. You bigger than most of them?"

"Nope, I'm one of the smallest, especially with the eighth and ninth graders out there. Is the drill ready to go?"

"Almost, I think. Don't worry. At least you're left halfback. The coach knows what he is doing."

"Are the weeds going to be bad anywhere?"

"Just some thistles around."

"Dad?"

"Yes."

"I'm not very good."

"How can you say that after just one day? Keep at it. A lot of good left halfbacks weren't even noticed in junior high school." In the silence that followed, Abe was glad for the activity of fixing the bend. Jimmy Charles interrupted, "There's a meeting of the football parents next Tuesday evening. You are supposed to go, if you want to."

"Your mother and I will go. You know how interested we are in you."

"Organized football is just about the last source of discipline in this country anymore." Coach Rambo stood in front of the auditorium and introduced the parents of the seventh grade boys to the game of football. The speech was more persuasive than it needed to be. Most of the parents—the natives, at least—agreed with him; but they needed to acknowledge approval, and he needed the experience of speaking in public. Coach Rambo was the heir apparent to Coach Rose's legend. Nobody ever mentioned it, because no one had ever really come face to face with Coach Rose's possible mortality; but if he ever did grow old and retire, Coach Rambo would still be there.

Coach Rambo was not exactly a native, but more native than transient. He had grown up about fifteen miles east of town, just across the district border, and had played at Moreland. After college, he came to Wheatheart where he assumed the assistant coach's role and drove home on weekends to help on the family farm. In addition to his duties as assistant farmer, assistant coach and high school history teacher, he coached the junior high team, but with Coach Rose's permission and supervision.

The parents knew this arrangement, so they listened indulgently as he made words come from a trembling throat. Though it was a good speech, he didn't seem to be too comfortable with it. It almost sounded as if he had read it in a book—something coaches should tell parents—but not at Wheatheart. Nevertheless, he continued.

"These young men are sure lucky to have a program like this. It will give them something to do. It will keep them out of trouble. It will teach them to get along when they have to. It will teach them to be tough, because we play tough football here at Wheatheart—always have and always will. And as we tell these young men, 'When the going gets tough, the tough get going.' That's true in every walk of life. You can look it up. Look at the great soldiers, the heroes of this great country. Most of those guys got their education running through those striped lines out there. You can help us help your boys become men, by encouraging them to play."

The parents nodded agreement. Their sons would have played without the speech. About the only boys who didn't play were a few transients who were small and the natives with Osgood Slaughter's disease, and they became managers.

Despite all this, Abe sat erect and looked as if he were listening with intensity. He had thought about this, had even rehearsed it in his mind. Through the method of remembering the future, he had researched the history of those in his position, and he had constructed a model for the father whose son plays left halfback. There was something about this role, and it was now time for Abe to fill it with the distinction it deserved. It was time for memory to turn to action. It was time to put off the feelings and frustrations of life as a pulling guard and move into the backfield of the community.

Shyness and hesitation weren't appropriate anymore. This role demanded a new character, something about halfway between confident and arrogant, but with humility. It was a delicate, demanding position. If he didn't play it right, the other parents' sons wouldn't block, and even the best left halfbacks needed blockers.

But Abe grew into the role as easily as he had grown into fatherhood. It wasn't all that unexpected. He had been remembering it for years. So as Coach Rambo spoke, Abe listened with mock intensity, conscious of the stares and envious glances which he sensed were coming his way. And he controlled himself. He controlled that fourteen-year-old urge to stand and shout to the top of the auditorium, to the top of the hill, to the top of the stadium itself, "My son is the left halfback!" Instead, he sat and wondered who was watching him as he listened.

Coach Rambo continued, mostly for the mothers, Abe thought. "Now if you have ever watched Wheatheart football, you probably already know what we do. It is just your basic game, mostly running with a pass thrown in to keep 'em honest." That was meant to amuse them, so they laughed politely as Coach Rambo waited for order. "Of course, Coach Rose and I have been talking this summer." This was meant to impress them. He wanted the patrons to get an image of his stopping his combine and rushing to town for an important meeting with the coach, sacrificing his harvest time for their sons. The audience didn't buy the image, but they forgave him for the effort. "We've been talking, and we think we might have grown a little stale." By now, Abe was getting impatient. It was difficult enough to maintain his role without this assistant apologizing for success. "We realized that we run to our right just a whole lot." Everyone knew that. Why should it surprise him. "And we think this year, we are going to mix it up more. Go back to the left a lot. We just don't want the opposition to think we have grown old and predictable."

This was meant to be amusing so the audience laughed even more politely than before—all except Abe. He feigned a smile befitting a man of his position, but he had to push it through the hard rock of disgust. What did Rambo mean? Wheatheart had always gone to the right. They weren't going to change now, not now. What did Rambo know? He was only an assistant, and he talked too much. Coach Rose never talked that much, and Coach Rose would continue to run to the right. For the first time in nearly a week, the vacuum came back to Abe's stomach; and he wanted to go home, to get away from the auditorium and the role he wore so he could sort through his remembering again. He wanted to go, but Mary Ruth, who had not really listened to any of the first part, was now sincerely intent. Coach Rambo had called in an eighth grader, the Brady boy, and was demonstrating the equipment, piece by piece. As usual he took too long and talked too much, so Abe hid behind his "halfway between confidence and arrogance" face, and remembered. He remembered the game—it would be with Canton—yes, the Canton game with their black and red uniforms, when Jimmy Charles would carry the ball a record thirty-five times for more than 300 yards.

Fall brought promise that year. The rains came in mid-September just as the maize heads began to fill. As gently as angel tears, as some of the rural women used to say, the rains fell off and on for almost five days. Each evening the ten o'clock weatherman would point to his maps and proudly announce the collected amounts in small towns across the state. It was a general rain, a multimillion dollar rain which came at the right time for everyone, except for some alfalfa farmers who should have had their hay in by now anyhow; and it seemed as if the weatherman wanted credit for it. But the rain was only part of the spirit of this fall. It wouldn't have seemed right for Abe to have planted his wheat seeds into the dry powdery dust, as he did in the fifties and early sixties. It wouldn't have been right for him to run his combine across the rough rows of scattered maize stubble gathering meager, shriveled heads as he had in years past. Poor farming would not have fit into the plan, not this year. This year there was too much joy, too much presence of the spirit which brings together right and good and bales them into one package.

In his head where his decisions were made, Abe had prepared for a dry fall. But in his heart where those decisions either stir the stomach or lie peacefully, he knew the rains would come. It is not something you tell someone. You don't brag about it at the John Deere place, and you don't spend valuable time redigging diversion ditches. But Abe knew it would rain, and he had made hidden preparations for it.

As soon as the fields were dry enough to support the tractor tires, Abe pulled his personal combination rig of tandem disc and drill from the barn and started putting the precious wheat seeds into the soil. But this year, it was different. Somehow, the sense of risk and gamble was gone. The maize heads in the nearby fields were full, the grains plump. The soil was the perfect texture, just the right red with the exact amount of moisture to nourish the small plants growing from the seed, without crusting the top surface. The world smelled prosperous. Across the horizon, the soil looked rich. In a matter of days, the sharp green of young living plants broke through the red soil and checkerboarded the whole countryside.

Although it was good, it wasn't as perfect for everyone as it was for Abe. Those farmers who had not tilled their seedbeds just before planting did get some crusting. The surface caked into an impregnable wall which turned the seedlings back into the soil instead of permitting them to spring forth into sunlight. There they rotted, and those farmers had to go through the expense and humiliation of reseeding.

The John Deere place provided the setting for public penance. Abe went as often as was prudent. Regardless of the participants gathered, he enjoyed the conversation.

"Got all your wheat up, Abe?" someone would eventually ask.

"Yep."

"Good stand?"

"Pretty good." He played it down for reasons of politeness. He had a good stand everywhere, but he didn't want to seem too proud. "What about you?"

"Nope. I had to resow nearly 200 acres. Just crusted over and I couldn't save it. Too wet, I guess. Did you pull that tandem disc in front of your drill again this year?" That was always a polite question. Everyone in the community knew how he sowed wheat.

"Yep."

"Well, I guess that was the right thing to do this year. Wish I had done it." This was an act of penance, this admission. In previous years, they had mocked him for his practice, "Too expensive. Too slow. Needless," they had said, but now they were apologizing.

Visibly, Abe accepted those apologies; but inside where he kept the feeling that his son was a left halfback, he judged them more harshly. "Transients," he thought. "That is not the way to farm. In this business, you decide what you have to do and do it that way every year. Sometimes it's right. Sometimes it's wrong. But you get old and broke trying to predict, trying to farm for a particular season. If we knew when and how it was going to rain, we would all be brilliant. So, you do what you do year in and year out and take the good with the bad. That's what it means to be a farmer. That's the code we live by." And he was glad for the season which caused him to confirm those thoughts.

That fall, the football was as good as the farming. After the third game, it bacame evident that the high school team was a state contender again. They had the combination of quality and depth which took the risk and chance out of the endeavor. The games were exciting, but it was excitement generated from seeing how things happened, how the team won, instead of whether it won.

For Abe and Jimmy Charles specifically, the seventh grade was a season of promise. Although he never played in a real game all season, Jimmy Charles suited up for the junior high games and ran plays from the left halfback position during the warm-up drills. There was nothing disappointing in this. The ninth graders were always so much bigger that no seventh grader ever played, ever intended to—except for Michael Garland who was on the kick-off team and caught punts. Nevertheless, the seventh graders had begun to play a part in the legend of Wheatheart football, and they took the role seriously.

Abe and Mary Ruth attended all the games knowing that Jimmy Charles would not play. This wasn't the issue. They were parents, and the code demanded that they become part of the total project, a part of the program. Their son was on the team. They had a duty. Actually, it wasn't that much of a sacrifice—it was only Monday nights, and the wheat sowing and maize cutting went smoothly in the spirit of prosperity. Jimmy Charles was even able to help out a ' lot after school and on Saturdays.

The Monday nights provided an opportunity for Mary Ruth to practice her "chatty mother in the stands" role; and they provided

Abe with enough real images that he could clothe his remembered images in lifelike uniforms. They always arrived at the games early enough for Abe to stand along the sideline and concentrate on Jimmy Charles' presence in the warm-up drills. Native that he was, Abe noticed every detail, the way the thigh muscles bulged in the back of the pants; the smooth, almost perfect stance; the eye forward with intent at the moment of handoff, rather than looking at the ball the way so many young backs do; the hip action through the hole; the cutting on the outside foot; the hustle back to the huddle after the play. To some, Abe's observations might have seemed just a silly game, but they were a necessary part of being the father of a left halfback. He had to observe these things. He would have corrected if correction had been needed. But he was satisfied. He would leave the coaching to Coach Rambo.

But during the long days as he pulled his tandem disc-drill combination through the isolated fields, he filled the spaces with those images remembered, now and future. One by one, on some days almost methodically, he remembered all the games to come and the role Jimmy Charles would play in each—a long run here, a touchdown catch in that one, a game-breaking punt return. Abe remembered it all, and as Jimmy Charles came sharper into focus in each scene, he was wearing his seventh grade face, seventh grade body, seventh grade moves. At first, the image amused Abe and he tried to change it, but he couldn't. The present was all he had to build his legend from, so he watched even more intently during warm-up drills the next Monday night. The plan had direction, and Abe was content to let it unfold. Only on rare occasions would he have to help it along.

One night during that precious time between going to bed and sleeping, Mary Ruth asked, "When do you plan to butcher the calf?"

Abe knew something was wrong. This was not proper conversation for this precious time. This was conversation suited for the dinner table or driving in the car or watching TV. He decided to wait.

"I don't know. Why?"

"Oh, we are short of meat; that's all."

That wasn't all, of course, but Abe decided to indicate that he had taken the hint by keeping the conversation going.

"How short?"

"Well, we're out of steaks." Despite Mary Ruth's frugal planning and meal budget, they always depleted the steak supply first. Being a farmer meant that you could eat "high on the hog" when you wanted to, but it also meant you had to eat everything else when the high parts were gone.

"So we'll have soup bone until I butcher?" Abe was teasing strongly and complaining mildly.

"It looks that way, I guess. It ought to be good enough for you. I don't see you losing any weight." Again she was stalling, but Abe had exhausted his supply of small talk on this subject so he had to wait.

By lowering her voice, she brought a reverence into the room darkened only by the absence of light. "Abe?"

"Yes?"

"Do you know who Mrs. Stevenson is?"

"I think so. Isn't she a sister-in-law to the Hoovers—moved in up on the river somewhere?" He was straining to get all the family history called into the conscious. Her quiz didn't demand that much research, but his standing as a native did.

"Yes, she's the one. She is doing some teaching up at school now."

He interrupted, "Substitute?"

"Yes, but I overheard her talking to someone in the grocery store the other day."

"Yeah?"

"And guess who they were talking about?" She hurried to the answer before Abe could get back into the process, "Jimmy Charles."

"Well?"

"Well," and she breathed a heavy sigh as if measuring the

consequence of what she was about to say, "she was just bragging on how smart he is and how much talent he has." She waited here for a comment, but went on in the following silence, choosing to keep the conversation herself. "She just went on and on about it." Again she hesitated as if to welcome any response which would shift the roles. "Abe, that woman has been around. She came from somewhere back East, Chicago, I think. She is just not comparing our son to Wheatheart. She is comparing him to children all over the country. And she still says those things about him." The pause that followed was for more refueling. "And she talked about him at the grocery store."

Abe knew that he finally was forced into speech, but he just couldn't think of the right thing. It was a bit like getting the exact thing you wanted at Christmas.The only thing to say sounds like the wrong thing. "Well, that was nice of her."

"Abe, it wasn't nice. That woman wasn't being nice. She didn't say those things to us. I just overheard her talking. She could care less about who we are. Abe, I tell you, that boy is something special."

"Well, sure he is. He is our son, after all."

"No, Abe. It goes deeper than that. It is almost as if he is too good to be our son."

Abe wouldn't tolerate that kind of talk, not even from his own wife. Even in his sense of security, there were too many moments of drought for him to let thoughts like that creep in. "Now, Mary Ruth, don't get carried away."

"Oh, I guess you're right. But mothers are supposed to get carried away."

Abe spent some time examining that statement. Mary Ruth was not like those dumb mothers who smother their kids with gifts and false glory. She could face the facts. It wasn't like her to get carried away, even with her own. No, her feeling deserved some attention.

She spoke again in the same reverent tones. "Abe, do you think he likes football?"

This gap was too big. Abe couldn't get from where he had been thinking to where he needed to be to respond to that statement. He couldn't contradict his earlier thought fast enough to consider the new one. His answer was too obviously hurried.

"Sure. Why do you ask?"

"I don't know. He just never seems to talk about it."

Abe breathed easier. The tone was changing, was returning to normal. "Well, he sure runs those plays with a lot of enthusiasm."

"Is he good, Abe?" She engineered the question with the skill of a wife. She would make him the expert, cast him into a distinctive father's role.

"Well, he's going to be. I can tell that."

She waited for a few minutes. "I would just hate for anything to happen to him. That's all. He just looks so little out there."

Without his realizing what she was doing, Abe read the cue and swelled into the role. "Sure, he's little against those ninth graders. You just wait. When he gets a little older, and plays against boys his own age, he's going to be all right. Just wait. You're going to be proud of him some of these days." Abe was pleased that he could share the results of his remembering with her, without revealing the actual process of remembering. He was pleased that he could sound so authoritative about that subject.

"I'm proud of him now," she answered softly.

They awoke when the light from the morning sun filled the room.

10

"I Sure Like Living!"
1978-1980

For Abe, Jimmy Charles' eighth grade year was like the seventh grade year, except better. The maize was good, the seedbed worked up moist and fine, and Jimmy Charles played a more active role on the team. This year he got to go down as an end on the kick-off team, a fact which pleased Abe. The end was a responsible position. The end man had to have the discipline to hold his place, not to get caught in fakes and not to be too eager to get into the glory of the play. The coach trusted Jimmy Charles—the boy had learned dependability from his father. He did what he was supposed to do. The coaches always commented about it. Abe would have been embarrassed if Jimmy Charles had not at least deserved the end position on the kick-off team. Perhaps he didn't make as many tackles as he would, had he been in the middle, but he had earned the respect of the coaches.

In addition to playing on the kick-off team, Jimmy Charles ran a few plays from left halfback in the games where the team had achieved a safe lead. There weren't many of these—although the junior high team was undefeated that season—but there were enough for Abe to perfect his role as father of a left halfback, enough for him to practice his remembering with feelings of reality. Every season, the possibility of this remembering was getting closer. Now he could fit into those scenes real bodies and real faces, real blockers blocking for real backs. His remembering was more serious now than it had been before. He had to be ready, at the John Deere place, at the Dew Drop Inn Cafe. It was not as if he were practicing moves or moods he would never use. He was preparing for real situations of the future. He was preparing for the day when the Ericsons became part of the left halfback legend.

Time moved quickly through the season and through the year. Jimmy Charles was at that awkward age physically, the time in development where the body is more than boy but not quite man. During the year, he spurted tall but not thick. His feet looked like oversized sleds mistakenly stuck on thin straight poles. His hands grew conspicuously large from the ends of his small arms. His voice was an experiment, always searching for correct timbre and pitch. Abe wasn't disheartened by this. He was amused and could laugh with Mary Ruth when they talked about it at night. Inside and alone, he was excited. Abe knew about this stage of growth. He had seen it in every animal he had ever raised. Calves have it, and dogs and colts. Even something as beautiful and graceful as a horse has to go through this stage of awkwardness. But animals—including sons—are not ugly at this stage. They are beautiful because this is part of the plan.

"I sure like living," Abe commented to Mary Ruth one night just after Jimmy Charles had started the ninth grade. He couldn't account for the statement. He had never actually thought it, not just that way; but he had filled a lot of spaces being grateful. Once he said it, he was glad he had made it public.

He had every reason to like living. He was preparing for a record maize harvest, the wheat was earlier and thicker than he had ever seen it before, and Jimmy Charles was a starter.

For both Abe and Mary Ruth, the junior high games were no

longer just parent responsibilities. They became events to be felt, absorbed. It was like the difference between going to church and going to a church dinner. Now the games were more than listening and watching and trying to cheer at the right times. They were experiences to be savored at the moment and digested later.

Mary Ruth sat in the stands, of course; but for the first time in her life, she really watched football. Abe took his usual position along the sidelines and invested about as much physical energy in the contest as the players did. The sideline rovers weren't as thick during the junior high games, so Abe could get right up against the restraining cable without being rude to anyone. From this proximity he was available for encouragement and frequent on-field coaching tips.

Jimmy Charles' play at left halfback was steady, occasionally brilliant. By now, Coach Rambo's remarks about running more to the left were two years old, and he and Coach Rose had forgotten them. This didn't surprise Abe or any of the other natives. A person can change his philosophy any time he wants to, but that probably won't alter the way he does things. For a while, Wheatheart did run to the left more, but that disappeared after a close call with Waynoka midway through the season. A new philosophy is all right until adversity comes, but then the stability of tradition conquers the flippant and fickle.

Jimmy Charles had no long, spectacular runs, but he had good gains. He found the open spaces; he followed the blockers; and he kept his weight forward. But he was particularly adept at blocking. The bird dogs noticed this quickly. At first, Abe was pleased as he stood along the sideline and overheard them point out Jimmy Charles' skill at this phase of the game. But later, he grew tired of their constant analysis. According to the bird dogs along the sidelines, Jimmy Charles blocked so well that he should be doing that every play. Occasionally, someone would forget that Abe was nearby, or would ignore it, and would yell, "Why don't you get that kid out of there and move him up on the line and let him block? Whoever told him he could carry the ball?"

Abe never said anything. He didn't know what to say. He had never realized that this was part of being the father of a left halfback; and he wondered if the other fathers who had filled this role before him had listened to this same foolish yelling from foolish fans. Probably so, and he had just not realized it. He wasn't going to let this destroy the present and the promise. But quietly he rejoiced that Coach Rose and Coach Rambo made decisions without consulting the bird dogs.

The junior high season was moderately successful—with only one blemish on the record. Alva beat them 12—8. Since there was not any scouting or much reporting at the junior high level, neither the players nor the fans ever really knew when to get up for a big game, so there wasn't any unusual buildup. Jimmy Charles had sowed wheat that weekend without mentioning the game. On Monday afternoon he had come home, completed his chores, and laid out his uniform methodically, just as he always did. The drive into town was typically quiet. Abe had remembered how important silence is to a player in those meaningful minutes and hours just before a game, so he held the time clear for Jimmy Charles. Abe did notice things along the way, the neighbors' progress in wheat sowing, the turning maize heads, coveys of quail that were using the last days before hunting season for gathering grain, the clear sky preparing itself for a full sunset. On normal days, he and Jimmy Charles could have made conversation about any of these things—Jimmy Charles was interested in all of it—but on game nights, Jimmy Charles was interested in only one thing.

Alva came out big and strong, and they played the game according to their talent. Their offensive drives were well-calculated four-yard runs built on other four-yard runs. On defense, they lined up in a tight six and just overpowered the Wheatheart line. Play after play, Jimmy Charles buried himself into the bigger opponents for no gain. Wheatheart's only score came on a broken play. Jimmy Charles, running a cross buck to the right, missed the handoff. Michael Garland, the quarterback, kept the ball and swept the end for sixty yards.

In the later stages of the game when the loss became evident, Abe suddenly realized that he was not prepared to help Jimmy Charles through this. It was, after all, his first loss since he had begun playing organized football. At this point, a father should be able to help his son. Criticism wasn't the answer. Jimmy Charles didn't need to be criticized. They had been beaten by a stronger team. These are the facts of life. He must accept that. But still, Abe wasn't sure how he could explain it to Jimmy Charles, so he stood and dreaded the final whistle and the subsequent ride home.

When the game ended, all the players reacted. Some stormed around in pretended anger. Some put on expressions of total dejection. Jimmy Charles took off his helmet, held it in the crook of his arm, and went over to talk with Coach Rose who had been standing behind the bench as if nothing more than a spectator. Abe shouted inside. Now the pressure was off. Coach Rose would talk to Jimmy Charles. This was his business, talking to football players after losses as well as wins. He would know what to say. He would know the delicate balance between letting Jimmy Charles know that it is not right to lose without making him dejected. Abe was glad for Coach Rose.

Still the ride home was as silent as the ride in, but this time the silence had a tension to it. All of them felt it, but no one seemed to want the responsibility for dealing with it. Finally, Jimmy Charles spoke. "Dad?"

"Yes?" Abe was cautious. He wasn't prepared.

"Did you see the Reinschmidt's new combine?" There was no remorse, no sadness in the voice.

Abe, still playing cautiously, responded, "No. What did they get?"

"A Gleaner." This was an interesting piece of information. Wheatheart was a John Deere town and any piece of new machinery which wasn't John Deere caused mild scandal.

Abe lowered his guard because of the significance of the present conversation. "Why did they do that?"

"I guess they had a lot of trouble with their old machine. Just got tired of repairing it."

"Well," Abe answered, "I really don't blame them. Reinschmidts are good farmers. They take good care of their stuff. There was something wrong with that machine from the start. Some people have had trouble with John Deeres which they brought on themselves, but not the Reinschmidts."

Suddenly Abe realized that the tensions had been broken. Jimmy Charles could now talk to his mother about the Civil War, his friendship with Mr. Benalli, the principal, a Brother Bob sermon, and eggs and chickens. The rest of the trip home went smoothly.

But as they neared the gate, Abe realized that avoiding the issue was a mistake. Jimmy Charles had suffered a loss tonight. Abe wasn't prepared to help him, but ignoring the question wasn't teaching Abe how to handle it, should it ever happen again. Abe had not fulfilled his father's task. He could forgive himself this time because he wasn't ready, but he had to be ready for the next time. He couldn't let this night pass without learning something.

"Jimmy Charles?"

"Yes?"

"Did you talk to the coach after the game?"

"I saw Coach Rose for a minute, but Coach Rambo didn't come in the dressing room."

Abe tried to produce a nonchalant attitude over a banging heart. "Oh, what did he say?" Abe would write the answer word for word and expression for expression in his memory so it would be his for the next time.

"He had read one of the poems I wrote, and we just talked about that."

Ninth grade graduation ranks second only to high school graduation as the social and cultural event of the year. There are bigger events—celebrations, pep assemblies on the night before the state championship and post-game trophy-presenting time in the gym on the Sunday afternoon after the championship game. At these events, the crowds are bigger and more active. The crowd is as important as the event, for every fan knows he had as much to do with the team's success as even the best player, and he claims his right to participate in the celebration.

But graduation is different. Graduation is significant, while football celebrations are only important. The crowd is sober. Although the principal, Mr. Benalli, always makes some announcement about the role parents have played in the student's education, the parents know that this success belongs to the child, that this event is his.

Graduations do attract crowds, though—parents, grandparents, and aunts and uncles who live within driving distance. The graduates themselves always make thorough plans about how they are going to spend the night with similarly victorious classmates; but when the event finally comes, there are usually so many relatives around that these plans die to code and duty.

Abe and Mary Ruth had spent about as much time preparing for Jimmy Charles' ninth grade graduation as they had spent preparing for the previous football season. Mary Ruth had invested some time in telephoning all the relatives within fifty miles, and Abe had invested some time in deciding how to wear his role as the father of the left halfback of the graduating class. That position halfway between arrogant and confident was a delicate one which demanded some practice.

For most Wheatheart boys, ninth grade graduation was the event of the first real suit. Some of the church families bought sports jackets and turtlenecks before then, but on this event the graduates would discover life from a formal perspective, wearing a complete suit with matching tie and shirt. Knowing this, Abe, Mary Ruth and Jimmy Charles completed the obligatory rituals early, traveling all the way to Enid to buy the suit before the graduation rush depleted the supply. Their efforts were rewarded. Jimmy Charles was handsome that night, and all the relatives said so.

Abe felt comfortably conspicuous as he sat with Mary Ruth in the middle of the section reserved for parents. Since the beginning of Jimmy Charles' football career, Abe was more conscious of people in crowds than he had been before. He was more conscious of them because they were more conscious of him. Rather than devoting himself to side trips of remembering, he had to stay loose and active, constantly glancing and listening. It was the difference between combining and plowing. When you plow, you can take those side trips. But in combining, you have to stay alert. Abe's public plowing days might have just ended, but he didn't mind.

The program itself was entertaining. Some more disinterested fans like ninth grade graduation programs even better than high school because there is more variety, a little humor mixed in with all the seriousness.

The class marched in one by one as Nancy Rogers played something slow on the piano. The crowd stood and watched intently; but each one, at least every native, stole a second of concentration from the marchers to wonder what the community would do when Nancy graduated and wasn't around anymore to play the piano at all the serious events. She was a valuable cog in community affairs, and they owed her a debt; but she wasn't going to be a schoolgirl forever. From history, they all knew that someone else would rise to the occasion when the time came, but they were still entitled to the opportunity to worry about it.

The procedure blended seriousness and silliness, the seriousness of the guest speaker—the Methodist minister, the awards, and the class song, combined with the silliness of the will and prophecy, written and delivered by students. During the awards part, Coach Rambo presented a medal to the most valuable junior high player. Abe knew about this and had prepared himself for it. For a while, he had thought they had a chance, he and Jimmy Charles; but after realistic evaluation, he had conceded the award either to Michael Garland, who was the most mature athlete on the team and the quarterback, or to Orville Schmidtz, the biggest player and one of the most promising tackles around. Either would be a fair choice, and he saw no conflict with his own role in this, not this time. After all, Jimmy Charles was still the left halfback.

As usual, Coach Rambo talked a little too long about the season, including the loss to Alva, and he took too long on the program to award the medal to Michael Garland. In doing so, he said the usual things—"One of the best young athletes we have ever had here; a young man who can rank right up there with the great ones in years to come; a real leader; a team player." When it was over, Abe applauded the selection and the speech as enthusiastically as anyone else; but in the midst of his applauding, Abe realized that he should learn something from this, in case he needed to practice it himself. So he turned in his seat to see how Scott Garland, the father of the most valuable junior high player, was receiving all this; but alas, Abe couldn't find him. There was his wife, Sue, but no Scott. He wasn't there. He had not even come. Later, Abe overheard Sue respond to the inevitable and seemingly courteous question which everyone was thinking with a casual, seemingly courteous, and meaningless put-off, "Oh," she responded to the question, "I guess he's off somewhere selling tractors."

Jimmy Charles won two awards, in addition to being the valedictorian of the class. Because of that honor, he was one of the principal speakers of the evening. His was the last speech, just before the benediction and the final prayer. When Mr. Benalli introduced him, he reported sincerely, "This young man is not only valedictorian of this class, but he is one of the finest students we have ever had at Wheatheart." In the quietness of the auditorium, Abe sensed that everyone agreed.

In his speech, Jimmy Charles intensely tackled the subject of individual independence. With his audience, he remembered some of the sturdy pioneers of the Wheatheart area, people like the Reinschmidts and the Walkers who had settled this country in the late years of the nineteenth century. He pointed out how these early settlers fought against disease and crop failure, how they had traveled all the way to Fort Reno—more than 180 miles round trip—to sell their crops and to buy supplies, how they survived the curse of the drought and dust storms and depression of the thirties, and how they had courageously sacrificed their young men to save the country during battle in World War II.

After enumerating these community achievements, he announced that these people had risen to the task because they were rugged, independent individuals who were not afraid to act out their own lives. He then challenged the whole audience, graduates and spectators as well, to be that kind of people. He concluded by reminding them that when God had created them, He breathed into each the breath of life. Each had been created with special attention; and to honor their Creator, each individual needed to seek his own unique purpose.

When Jimmy Charles finished and returned to his seat, a momentary hush more serious than the already serious tone of the event fell across the auditorium. Then suddenly, the crowd burst into loud applause which would have been appropriate following a gallant touchdown run, but seemed even more honest and more appreciative here.

Abe tried to fight the discomfort he was celebrating in his total being by fidgeting for his handkerchief, but Mary Ruth handed him the one she had already used to wipe away her scattered tears.

After the benediction and the final parade of the graduates toward the exit, a long line of congratulators formed to wait their turn to thank Jimmy Charles for his speech. The community had never heard a graduation speech quite like that, where the speaker had used the home folks for his heroes. Usually, the speakers quoted Cicero or Lincoln or Glenn Cunningham or someone famous. These home folks had suddenly become stars in the drama of reality and persuasion, and they liked the attention. Whether they had heard the challenge or not, they had at least heard the illustrations.

Abe studied that long line carefully. He studied each face and each personality, and he remembered his life's interaction with each. He particularly noted those in the line who had come to shake his hand on that day years ago when a wild and reckless Abe and Mary Ruth had dedicated their son in the front of the Baptist church.

Near the end of the line, patiently waiting his turn to speak to Jimmy Charles, stood Coach Rose. Coach Rose attended every graduation and almost every play and concert, but he always sat in the background. Anyone who saw him had to make an effort. But here he stood now, awaiting his turn to congratulate a ninth grader who had not even begun varsity football yet.

For Abe it was a strange sight. He remembered all the times he had stood in line to speak to the coach—to get a piece of tape, to check on a bruise or a blister, to turn in dirty sweat socks, or to get his letter or district champion patch. There weren't many men for whom Abe would stand in line, but Coach Rose was one of them. In fact, he was at the head of the list; and now the man at the head of his list was waiting in line to speak to Abe's own flesh.

11

That's What Sons Are For
1980 - 1981

On the Oklahoma plains, summer ends early for the varsity football player. Two-adays begin on August 15. While the rest of the folks are still complaining about sweltering sun rays and dry southern winds and are planning outdoor cookouts and swimming parties, the young men of the community—at least the gallant ones—shuck off the frivolity and casualness of summer and plant the serious seeds of fall nights and football.

Despite the early morning starts and late evening finishes, they endure pain, thirst, sweat, frustrations, put-downs and build-ups, and hopes. The classic Spartan waterless and bloody practices have long since disappeared, taking their place in history with high top shoes, leather helmets, and the single wing offense. Coaches now regulate liquid consumption and monitor weight loss with the same professionalism they use when conducting tackling drills and controlled scrimmages.

Nevertheless, football practice is a time of trial, a time of learning. The successful players, those who catch the coach's eye, push their bodies beyond the mental limits of hurt, and they sear over their emotions with the fire of purpose. They run farther and faster than they really want to. They close their eyes, bang their bodies into other bodies, and try to ignore the impact. They lick salty perspiration deposits from the corners of their mouths and wipe their eyes with gritty shirt tails. They concentrate on intricate geometric maneuvers while thirst dulls their minds. When the insides of their heads pound and throb reaction against all the cruelty, they wear their helmets even when resting, because the coach said to wear them.

Through this process, boys become men. Street-wise wimps and mothers' precious babies become warriors worthy to wear the green and white onto the field of honor. It is a necessary process, but it is more than that. It is patriotic; it is religious.

In Wheatheart, as in other towns, the demands of the two-adays are such heavy commitments that the players don't have much time for other activities. About the only luxury is the postpractice meetings at the Whippet Drive-In where the players consume giant portions of the house specialty, cherry limeades. By now, the postpractice meetings and even the drink are part of the ritual, but so is the justification. The seniors initiate the sophomores by telling them, "We've got to get our vitamin C." At the drive-in, the players, mostly barefoot and in shorts, drape themselves on and in their cars and entertain high school girls (who also know the ritual) with recounts of the practice—always making it harsher than it really was.

As a sophomore, Jimmy Charles became a part of all this. It was almost as if he had been drafted into the army. He disappeared early each morning, came home to nap, went back in the evening, and returned home just in time to get in bed, in preparation for another day. Since Mary Ruth did not fully understand all the feelings and the memories and all the pride involved, she resented the process— the time demands and the fatigue her son had to endure. But Abe, because he knew, enjoyed it. His only regret was that he could not move inside Jimmy Charles' body and soul and experience it all just as his son was. He had heard a word once, and he looked it up in the dictionary one night when no one was watching. There it was—*vi-*

car-i-ous (adj.), "to feel as if one were actually taking part in what is happening to another." That described it for him. He did drive by the practice field every time he went to town, but he felt it would be too obvious for him to stop very long. For now, he would be content to remember and feel vicariously.

When school started, two-adays ended; but the one remaining practice, beginning just after school, extended longer into the evening. On the second day, Jimmy Charles came out to the wheat field as soon as he got home from practice. By then, the sun had turned its fierce color onto the western horizon. The heat waves which had played across the plowed and baked ground all afternoon had disappeared; and a coolness, not pronounced but significant, had settled on the plains. Even the tractor responded to the difference. The motor purred with a smoothness which had not been there during the hotter parts of the day, and Abe no longer had to shift into a lower gear to pull the sweeps through the spotty patches of clay.

Jimmy Charles took his old seat on the tool box and rode alongside Abe as he used to years ago, before he had become a man himself. It had been a long time since the two of them had been in that position—Abe driving and remembering and Jimmy Charles riding and watching. Both enjoyed it—this chance to return to the security of a former good time. The cool evening breeze, the smooth-running tractor turning the glistening red soil, and the companionship of father and son riding side by side into lengthening shadows, blended into a perfect mixture of peace and progress.

The two accented the silence with occasional conversation, made briefer and more direct by the necessity of talking above the tractor purr. They covered familiar subjects, everyday topics important only to them. They discussed the clay patches, some scattered bindweed in another field, an oil leak in a tractor axle, the new tractor a river farmer had just bought, seed wheat, and combine repairs. These were mutual topics which they needed to discuss, and Abe was glad for the opportunity. Yet, there was a more profound topic which Abe chose not to mention, fearing it might not be as mutual as the others. So they rode in the security of silence and safe remarks.

"Dad?" Jimmy Charles broke another period of fruitful silence.

Abe sensed that this was different from the others. Like the cool breeze which was subtle but significant, this lead was cooler than the previous ones. Instead of answering, he saved his throat until he could determine the new direction.

Jimmy Charles continued, "Can you get all the wheat sowed by yourself this fall?"

"I guess so. Why?"

"Well, I won't get home until pretty late, with football practice."

"I know." Abe had been used to that kind of thoughtfulness for a lot of years by now, but it still surprised him when it came. Here was a young man in the midst of his one great experience in life, and he was worried about the farming. Abe knew there was a plan—he had known that for a long time; but he often wondered why he had been chosen to have such an unselfish son.

Jimmy Charles continued a mild protest of the ethics of the plan. "But it just doesn't seem right, leaving you here with all this work to do."

Abe mustered the confidence often required of fathers and answered matter-of-factly, "I'll manage."

Jimmy Charles let the threat of darkness penetrate both their thoughts for a few minutes before he replied, "But if you get behind, I could always quit."

"No," was all Abe could say. He wanted to say more, to thunder protests louder than the tractor roar and darkness, to explain life and meaning and importance and significance. He wanted to relate years of remembering moment by moment, detail by detail, run by run, and touchdown by touchdown. He wanted to do all that, but he couldn't. For one thing, there were tears in his throat, and he couldn't speak. But at a level underneath those tears where he could just barely reach, he couldn't answer because he didn't understand. Unselfishness is a noble quality, but where is the boundary line between unselfishness and foolishness? Can a person become so considerate that he actually becomes selfish in his attempt not to be?

When does what is right butt against what is good?

At this level, Abe pondered fatherhood. He wondered why it had to be so complex. If Jimmy Charles smoked or drank, it would have been a lot easier. Abe could have lectured about those things. He could have set the line and held it straight. He could have been as convincing about those things as Brother Bob. He could have insisted and demanded. But how do you deal with too much unselfishness? Where do you set that line? He decided he couldn't, so he chose to treat the incident as Jimmy Charles' attempt at humor, nothing more. But he couldn't forget the night. It was too pleasant and too unbearable.

Abe didn't get too far behind that fall. He did have to start a little earlier and stay in the fields a little later, but he managed to get the wheat sowed, the maize harvested, the stubble plowed, and the high school team cheered through another state championship.

As expected, Jimmy Charles played on the kick-off team and in runaway games. Sophomores usually don't play that much, even those who have the physical size and strength. Football is too complicated to be entrusted to the immaturity of a sophomore, of a student still too young to drive an automobile legally. Abe knew this; the town knew this; so there was nothing unexpected, for parents or players. Michael Garland and the Schmidtz boy did play. In fact, they both became starters before the season was over, but they were exceptions. The rule was that sophomores played on the kick-off team and in runaway games. It had always been that way. They play just enough to feel a part of the successes and to keep their appetites whetted for the final two high school years when they would become men on the football field as well as in other places.

Since it was a season of immediate expectation, the sophomore year went fast. Despite the year of limited action, Abe was still the father of a left halfback; and he had a duty to fulfill.

Although it went fast, this was still a strange year and a full one. For one thing, the team won the state championship. The Whippets, with Jimmy Charles yelling encouragement from the bench and Abe watching and remembering his plan from his spot along the sidelines, marched through ten regular season wins and four play-off games without a blemish or so much as a poor performance. It was all a methodical, calculated procedure, just as if it had been planned to perfection by some force bigger even than Wheatheart.

Through an unusual set of circumstances, Jimmy Charles almost got to play a larger role than Abe would have liked this early in his career. On the Monday before the state championship game, Bobby Golden, who started at left halfback in front of Jimmy Charles, got into a fight with Charlie Brady's grandson. Right in the middle of the hall during the period just after lunch, they banged away at each other. Throughout the afternoon, as news reports leaked out the high school door and down the hill into the heart of town, the citizens held their breath, wondering how it would all be resolved.

In other schools, fighting in the hall might not be a big deal, but it was in Wheatheart. You fought on the football field. You obeyed the rules in school. Everybody knew that, all the townspeople, and all the students, including Bobby Golden and Charlie Brady's grandson. This was serious, all right, fighting in school; and the citizens who felt a community responsibility to evaluate the decisions, even when they couldn't make them, wondered how it would work out.

If the school officials took the hard line and suspended the two boys for such a crime, both would surely be ineligible for the state championship game; then the substitutes, Jimmy Charles in particular, would play.

By late afternoon, the latest news flash filtered down the hill and spread rapidly. Mr. Benalli and Coach Rose had worked out a suitable punishment. The culprits would have to run extra laps in practice. The community breathed a sigh of relief. The town hope and prestige still rested on the best Wheatheart had to offer, instead of on a sophomore second-stringer.

Even Abe breathed easier when he heard the news. He could have managed the idea of having Jimmy Charles play in that game, all right. But it was still too early. The plan had not called for stardom during the sophomore year, and Abe was in no hurry to rush the plan. He could wait, because he somehow knew the right time was still coming.

The next morning, Abe got up early and went into the town to eat breakfast at the Dew Drop Inn. Mary Ruth asked about that strange behavior, with fresh eggs and ham right at his own table, and Abe managed a flimsy excuse—he wanted to get a load of feed before the line got too long at the Co-op. Since Mary Ruth didn't know how long the lines were at the Co-op, she had to accept that as a reason, but she still wondered.

And she had a right to wonder, because Abe wasn't even sure himself. It was something he had to do, but he didn't know why. He knew the early morning crowd at the cafe included Mr. Benalli, as well as the usual traffic of semiserious eaters and serious talkers. And he knew the conversation would eventually get around to that fight and the punishment. And he knew that Mr. Benalli, representing the school, would be put on a spot. Although everyone in town was glad for the decision which was made, and was glad because Bobby would still play, not everybody agreed with it.

"The school is getting too lenient."

"Fights are going to break out all over the place."

"Benalli's been up there so long he doesn't even care anymore."

"They gotta crack down on those kids before things get out of hand and we ain't no different from the big cities."

The evaluations would run thick and frequent all day and maybe even until Friday when Bobby Golden would redeem himself in the state championship game and everyone would forget the incident.

Abe knew how the town would react, and he wanted to get there early. Actually, if anyone had a right to protest, to be angry, he did. He had the most to lose. Since Bobby was going to play, his dad and not Abe would sit overdressed and cocky at the big celebration assembly at the school gym on Sunday afternoon.

But Abe wasn't angry, because he knew there was a plan. He wanted Mr. Benalli to know that. He wanted those people in charge to know that they had his support, Benalli, Coach Rose, and Casteel, the weird old superintendent. He wanted them to know that he respected their judgment. Abe was pleased with that respect, for to him it was a matter of faith. When you know there is a plan, you can respect the judgment of those along the way.

So Abe went to breakfast and lent his silent support to Mr. Benalli and the decision which had been made. It was his civic duty, and what he wanted to do.

With Bobby playing only fair on Friday, the team won anyhow and Bobby's father acted the big shot on Sunday afternoon. Abe watched it all from a distance and was only slightly envious, but in a satisfied sort of way.

That winter the oil boom hit Wheatheart; well, it almost hit. At least the mania hit and caused a minor stir. Those towering derricks which a few years ago had dotted the scenery of adjacent communities moved to the edges of the Wheatheart area, and the town began to prepare for the oncoming activity and wealth.

Some people, mostly transients, fell comfortably into the oil pattern. They started to talk in a strange new language, using words which only they could understand, words which either shut the farmers out or forced them to learn the new language and maybe, eventually, a new lifestyle.

Abe chose not to do it, and Mary Ruth commended him for his decision. Even when the oil men came with offers to lease his land for drilling prospects, Abe chose not to take their offers. He didn't want anyone punching holes in his land, gambling on what might be buried beneath it. He enjoyed growing crops on top of it too much. Sure, that was a gamble too, but Abe knew that risk and he understood it.

When the neighbors and townsmen borrowed money and bought trucks and forklifts and went to work in the oil fields, Abe plowed, repaired his machinery, did the chores, and waited for harvest, just as he had every year of his adult life.

With all the oil talk that winter, Abe began to feel something like a transient right in his own town. But that feeling didn't last long. Too many of the wells around Wheatheart were either dry or weak; so in a few short months, the oil men shook the mud of Wheatheart off their boots and took their rigs elsewhere. The gamblers lost huge chunks of money on equipment they had bought; but at least the Dew Drop and John Deere conversation once again concentrated on wheat prices, weather, Washington, and football. And once more, Abe enjoyed going to town and being the father of the next left halfback.

In the spring, Jimmy Charles received even more fame, statewide fame this time, but it was all so strange that Abe had a hard time understanding or appreciating what was happening. Jimmy Charles won state awards for his poetry.

Mr. Benalli, the principal, sent the poems in. He, himself, had had something of a rough winter. At one point, he thought about leaving Wheatheart; then he got pneumonia from jumping into Wagner's pond and rescuing Craig Brady and Bobby Golden. During all this time, Jimmy Charles developed a rather close friendship with this adult in need. But it was more than a friendship. It was more like the relationship Jimmy Charles had with Coach Rose. It seemed, at least to Mary Ruth, and to Abe when she told him about it, that Jimmy Charles meant more to the adults, both the coach and the principal, than some of the other adults in town did. These men found something in their son which was important to them.

So Mr. Benalli, either out of friendship or out of a desire to give Wheatheart more attention than just football, or out of a need to feel important himself, sent some of Jimmy Charles' poetry to a committee that judged such things.

Jimmy Charles won, but not just once. Several of his poems were voted the best in their respective categories, categories based on things like whether the poems rhymed or not. Mary Ruth understood it all, but Abe didn't. He just knew Jimmy Charles won. And

145

he was proud of Jimmy Charles, really proud; but he never mentioned it down at the John Deere store, and he was glad nobody else did.

But the Wheatheart Garden Club mentioned it. Those were the ladies such as Doc Heimer's wife and Mrs. Casteel who had taken it upon themselves to bring culture and beauty to Wheatheart. Usually, they took care of Memorial Day plans out at the cemetery and planted wild flowers near the overpass on the highway and helped groom some Wheatheart girl for the Miss County Fair contest.

But now that Wheatheart had its own poet, those ladies appointed themselves the job of planning a fitting celebration. Just like the state championship football celebration, the event took place on a Sunday afternoon at the high school gym. But the similarities ended there. No fans showed up, only a few teachers, the Garden Club, and the students in the English classes who might have been bribed into coming on the promise of extra credit.

This time Jimmy Charles was not just part of a crowd being honored. He was the only one, and he handled himself as if he was even comfortable with all the attention.

The program was simple. Mrs. Foster, the high school music teacher, sang a song with a tape recording for accompaniment; Jimmy Charles read his poems; Mr. Benalli presented Jimmy Charles the trophies he had won and made a rather interesting speech about what a rare person he was; and Mrs. Heimer announced a long list of Garden Club projects and then urged everyone to mingle.

To top it off and make the event different, the ladies served refreshments—hot tea and cheese sandwiches cut into eighths. During it all, Abe sat in a corner, trying to balance several of those little sandwiches and trying to remember if he had ever had hot tea before. Sure, he had had iced tea, maybe every day of his life, but he could never remember drinking tea while it was still hot. Although he hoped no one saw him, some did and came by to congratulate him for raising such a son. But all their good words only made his neck sweat. He knew how to be the father of the starting left halfback. He had practiced that. For years, across acres and acres of plowing and sowing and combining, he had practiced that. But he had never practiced anything like this, and he didn't know what to do except to sit there and look out of place with a cup of hot tea in his hand.

On the other hand, Mary Ruth fit in well that day. She probably had never had hot tea before either, but she knew people drank it and she drank it as if she knew how. Afterward, she took all those poems home, glued them to some old shingles she had saved when they tore down the Cole house, and decoupaged them. When she hung her new treasures in exactly the right spots throughout the house, she did it all with such purpose and design that Abe got the idea that she had thought about this before.

That idea scared Abe a bit. While he had been remembering success all these years, Mary Ruth's remembering had been active too, but focused on different matters.

At first, Abe wondered how they could put their remembering and planning together, but then he decided they didn't need to, not with Jimmy Charles, at least. Next, he tried to think like Mary Ruth and tried to remember what it meant to be the father of a state champion poet, but he had no background for it. Besides, summer was coming and soon it would be fall and football season again.

Early summer was a busy time for Abe and Jimmy Charles and the rest of Wheatheart area farmers. It was time made busier by variety and ambiguity. When the farmers had something to do—harvesting, plowing, planting—they could define their objective and check their progress day by day. They were busy during those times, but it was a contented busyness. However, during early summer, they were busy and they couldn't understand why for sure. There were so many odd and endless jobs that they never really had the feeling they had accomplished anything. There were fences to fix, scattered maize patches to replant, some weed patches to plow up, fence rows to mow, combines to repair—an endless procession which never ceased but just faded away when harvest and purpose finally returned the world to normal by mid-June.

In the midst of this suspended purpose, Abe often thought impulsively; and on rare occasions, he even acted impulsively. This early summer, he decided to buy a new springtooth. He had not discussed it with Mary Ruth at all, and had only mentioned it to Jimmy Charles; but he set his mind one night before bedtime and made his move early the next morning.

By eight o'clock when he arrived at the John Deere place, it was already a circus of activity. The main attraction was Scott Garland's smashed automobile which had been dragged to an out-of-the-way but now popular corner of the machinery yard. It was severely damaged. All the metal along the right side was battered and cracked. The right front wheel was bent backward. The guts of the automobile showed through gaping holes, and all the glass had been shattered. Abe was struck with its ugliness. He liked automobiles, as much as he liked any other piece of machinery. He found them fascinating and often beautiful. But he suddenly realized that he liked them when they were perfect, standing sleek and trim, waiting to be driven, to be used. This car was ugly, with its raw material exposed and distorted, sitting there like a freak in a sideshow. The beauty was gone, and Abe couldn't look at it for long without getting nauseous, so he turned away and gathered the details.

Since car crashes are big news in Wheatheart, the bystanders could provide a colorful and colored accent. Michael, Scott's son, was driving a carload of boys. . . . seven miles south of town on the county road. . . . slid on some loose gravel and went out of control and hit the Beaver Creek bridge. . . . none of the boys are hurt bad, but a lot of cuts. . . . the Schmidtz boy had a broken arm. . . . Michael had fifty stitches in his face. . . . about midnight last night. . . . just lost control when it slid on some loose gravel. . . . wasn't going too fast. . . . really lucky. . . . if they had been going faster, woulda killed them all. . . . heard the ambulance going out. . . . lots of blood there in the car. . . . three of them had to have stitches. . . . all had been released from the hospital already.

. . . just lost control. . . . loose gravel will get you. . . . just start slipping and can't stop. . . . lucky they weren't going fast. . . . car's a total loss, all right. . . . slipped on some loose gravel and hit the Beaver Creek bridge.

This was the official report. It would be recorded in annals of Wheatheart history to be remembered for at least two decades, depending on how long Scott left the ugly reminder sitting in the machinery yard. This was the official report which would be carried on the front page of the *Wheatheart Journal* and in town conversation. The unofficial one, the real one, would be believed but never discussed. Although everyone thought it, no one would ever mention the recklessness, the speed, the alcohol, the reason why five sons of leading citizens were anywhere near the Beaver Creek bridge at midnight.

In the confusion of it all, Abe tried to sort through his range of responses for the correct one. He was glad that none of the boys was hurt badly—at least, he thought he was glad; but he was also glad in a proud sort of way that Jimmy Charles was not involved and would never be involved in such nonsense. He wanted to feel sorry for Scott and the other fathers, but he wanted those fathers to return his sympathy with envy—just a little envy at least.

He tried to interpret this event from a sense of justice and within the character of the order which made things happen as they did. These boys were football players; two were starters. Coach knew the reason for the accident, the real reason. He would have to know. In his silence, he could squint his eyes and see through any mask. He could tell when one of his boys was just thinking about getting into trouble, and he could speak that idea right out of existence. Now that the act was done, he would have to deal with it. But how? Would he punish the boys? Or ignore their crime against the community? Would he, early next season in his customary manner of acting without explaining, simply move Jimmy Charles ahead of all these guys? After all, Jimmy Charles had not slipped on loose gravel and driven into the Beaver Creek bridge. He could be trusted. But hadn't these five violated their right to be trusted with community honor? What was just? What was right? And did that conflict with what was good? Abe didn't know, so he was happy that Coach Rose had to deal with it.

Scott Garland came out of the store when he sensed that Abe was a buying customer instead of just another passionless student of automobile wrecks. Without referring to the accident, Abe communicated his need (or his impulse), and together they inspected the display of springtooths until they found the right one for Abe's needs. After the customary price dickering, small talk, and kicking tires and metal, they came to an agreement, and the transaction was made.

"If we pump this tire up, I think you can just pull this thing behind your pickup, Abe," Scott assured him, as if afraid that Abe might change his mind.

"No," Abe answered, "I'll send Jimmy Charles in with the tractor." He paused for a while as if weighing the appropriateness of his next statement in his present company, but confessed anyway, "I just hate to pull machinery on the highway. Always have. I'll send Jimmy Charles instead."

Scott laughed what might have been a sincere laugh, "Well, I guess that's what sons are for, to do what the old man can't do."

Charlie Brady, who had witnessed the whole transaction while perched on a nearby tractor seat, added, "Or never could."

All this struck Abe as funny and he laughed about it then and when he remembered it during the harvest weeks that followed.

12

The Whole World Is Transient

1981

In late July, Abe made another eventful trip to the John Deere store, although that was not his original destination. He had come to town to supplement Mary Ruth's grocery supply so she could delay shopping for another two weeks. Again, he came early, just after eight o'clock. He was going to get into the store and right back home so he could rest Jimmy Charles from the plowing for a couple of hours. But when Abe pulled his pickup onto Main Street, he sensed that something was amiss. He couldn't tell what it was, but something wasn't right this morning. Suspecting fire, he inventoried all the physical structures and eliminated that possibility. The activity on the street—some senior citizens out for the morning constitutional and the pickup trucks in front of the Dew Drop Inn—was not unusual, but something was out of order. He tried to remember last night's news, thinking perhaps there was a national issue, war or something. But this was bigger than national news. This was Wheatheart news, and he had to get the official report; so he made a U-turn at the old picture show and drove to the John Deere place.

When he walked in, he could tell it wasn't good. The crowd,

larger than usual for a plowing day, had gathered in front of the giant water fan; and the spirit was as clammy as the atmosphere.

"What happened?" Abe asked someone standing on the periphery.

Art Garland, sitting in his office cubicle, overheard and answered with a bit of a sigh, "Rose quit last night."

"What?" Abe was still gathering information and had not yet begun to sound shocked.

Someone else supplied the details Art had not included. "The coach submitted his resignation to the school board last night."

Another bystander recounted for Abe, himself, and the rest of the crowd further notes. "He's going to coach one more year; then he's going to quit—coaching that is. Stay on as a teacher, I guess."

Art asked no one in particular, "What would happen if we told him he can't stay if he won't coach?"

The whole crowd was shocked. Art shouldn't have said that, even if he thought it. The coach can do what he wants to. With a lesser man, that might have been a good idea, but not with Coach Rose.

Although he had nothing to say, Abe had to say something. He was not prepared to explore this in his mind, and he could delay the operation so long as he stayed in the conversation. "Who's going to take his place?"

"Rambo, I guess."

"He'll do all right."

"Yeah, but he ain't Rose."

"That's for sure."

"But who is?"

"You can say that again."

"That man is a walking football machine. That's all he ever thinks about."

"If you could think as good as he can, you could spend your life thinking about football too."

"I guess you're right."

"He sure has given us some memories."

"A lot of good ones."

Art was still cantankerous. "I don't know. Maybe our basketball will get better now." On normal occasions, that would have redirected the conversation, but not this morning. Art was out of calibration, and the flow went on despite him.

"How long has Coach been here?" someone asked in continuation.

"Thirty-one years." A few moments of silence followed this reminder as the participants chased their favorite memories through those thirty-one years.

"Well, life goes on," Art reminded them.

"Sure won't be the same."

"The man is a football genius, all right."

"Thirty-one years. . . . football genius. . . . all he ever thought about. I remember when. . . . District Championship game. . . . all-staters. . . . State Championship game. . . . thirty-one years. . . . the man had a one-track mind. . . . Well, at least we had him—think of the people who have never had him. . . . best in the business. . . . won't be the same. . . . thirty-one years." The conversation went round and round until it made Abe dizzy. He had to face the inevitable. He had to think about this. So he completed his mission and went home.

Jimmy Charles took the news easily. "I know there are a lot of other things he wants to do with his life, and I'm glad he's finally going to do them."

Abe didn't understand that, but he hadn't understood a lot of things Jimmy Charles had said about the coach or things the coach said about Jimmy Charles. He decided not to let their strange talk interfere with what he knew was right, so he put it aside to deal with his thoughts.

When he worked through all this, it was easy for him to conclude and announce to himself, almost aloud, "Well, it won't make that much difference. It's only a year. Jimmy Charles is already located in position. He is the left halfback. The team already has the start. Rambo is a good man, maybe even as good as Rose in some ways. We will make the most of this year, and let the next year take care of itself. At least, Rose will be here one more year."

Those are the things he told himself, but he wasn't convinced. It was like the time when Jimmy Charles was in the first grade and brought home the mumps. Abe's mother took that opportunity to remember that Abe had never had them. Somehow, during boyhood, he had escaped. Mary Ruth only laughed knowingly. Abe wanted to defy her smugness, and every morning he would get up feeling good and say, "I think I'm going to miss them." But inside where all men contract order, he knew better. So he did his chores, pretended he had made it through safely, and waited to get sick.

Of course, three weeks later he did come down with the mumps, just as people said he would. He spent the next two weeks lying around the house boring himself and bothering Mary Ruth, and also realizing that the inevitable always comes, regardless of what you do before it gets there.

This time, he told himself it wouldn't make any difference if the coach had quit; but he still had the same feeling as when he was waiting for the mumps to come.

The news of Coach Rose's resignation burned through the late summer sun and the hot dry southern winds, making the whole season arid and barren. In early August, the maize stalks quit growing almost immediately, as if they were on strike to protest an absense of water. The soil which was to be the bed for the precious wheat seeds turned to powdery silt and lay thirsty under the heat waves which danced overhead.

Town conversation focused on, "It's sure dry," and "At least, he's going to stay another year," but there was doom in everyone's voice. These people had been through dry seasons before. They knew how one started; and even though it's chancy to predict the weather, they knew that they were in for a spell. No one would be surprised when it happened. In the face of this impending doom, there was only one thing to do—keep on with life. So the farmers continued to till the seedbeds and prepare the combines for harvesting the maize which was rapidly burning to nothingness under the oppression of each day's sun. And the young warriors started two-adays.

Once more, Jimmy Charles went through the ritual. This time he was a junior, well past the learning period and the bench sitting. Now he was ready for action; he and his fellow players who practiced in the dry dust tried to forget their fathers back home plowing the dry dust.

If any of them could have foreseen the future, the farmers and the football players, they might have altered some things. But that's part of the excitement, not being able to see how it is all going to come out, but still knowing that this cycle will come and go, just as all the others before it have. In the meantime, you make this day look like yesterday. Since you don't know what tomorrow is going to look like, the present is based on the past. Politicians and book writers talk about preparing for the future, but that's silly talk. You don't know where you are going, but you do know where you have been, and it wasn't all that bad. So you keep on doing the things you know to do and wait until it starts raining again. That's the code of the prairie.

Jimmy Charles came home from the evening practice and went out to the field where Abe was mixing dry dirt with dryer dirt. He climbed aboard the tractor and took a position on the tool box. It was like the evening they had spent this way last year, but it was different. This time, the soil was too fine and Jimmy Charles' attitude was too dry. Abe sensed the difference, but he chose to let things ripen naturally.

Jimmy Charles spoke first. "Looks like tea."

"What?"

"That dirt looks like tea, a wild, red tea of some kind."

"Maybe so." Although he never expressed it, Abe often appreciated Jimmy Charles' imagination.

"Does red corn make red meal?"

"What?"

"I was thinking it looked like red corn meal."

That one was funny, and Abe laughed a bit. The dirt did look like red corn meal, and the thought amused him. "Maybe we can live on mud pies." He enjoyed the humor, but he wanted to make sure that Jimmy Charles fully understood the seriousness of the season. It occurred to him that in sixteen years, Jimmy Charles had never known anything but rainy years, had never lived anything except rainy years and Coach Rose's football.

"Dad." The tone was dry. The word had sprung from a tense, parched throat and poured over sun-baked lips.

"Yes?"

"I've been moved."

Abe turned in the tractor seat and watched the implement discs sift the soil, raising it high in the air and letting it float back to its resting place. He watched, but he didn't see. There were no tears, but there were cracks in his forehead as he contemplated his fertile lagoons, his lifetime oasis disintegrating into barren mirages. Momentarily, he tried to prepare himself for the worst. For more than sixteen years, Jimmy Charles had been a left halfback, in all of the remembering and in all of the reality. How can you cancel that out in an instant and rewrite it with something new and transient which could never be as rewarding? He thought of the possibilities. Fullback—no he's too slow for that. Quarterback—not likely, though the coach likes him, but in a different sort of way. Tight end—maybe so, and that wouldn't be too bad. It's a step down, but Abe thought he could adjust. Jimmy Charles would be visible on the end, could utilize his blocking, and still figure on the offense with some passes. Tight end was a poor substitute, but it was better than nothing, Abe decided. "Where?"

Jimmy Charles took his turn to study the sifting soil. "Offensive center."

Abe's physical machinery operated the tractor automatically, but his insides turned into dry dust, and he tasted that thirst in his mouth that water couldn't quench. Abe, himself, had been a pulling guard. At least that had some visibility on some plays. And there had even been some pulling guards who had gone down in the legend books. Abe could remember three or four. But trying hard, he could not recall one single offensive center either on the field or in town talk. The position was just one of those necessary non-roles that someone has to do in life, like working on an assembly line. Offensive center. The words pounded his brain into an ache. He was not angry. He was obliterated. Although he tried to fill his voice with some moisture, the words were still lifeless. "Gonna play there?"

Jimmy Charles tried to be optimistic for both of them. "I think so. I block pretty good, and I can make the long snap on punts."

Abe remembered that making the long snap was important. The feat wasn't so much a matter of talent as a matter of discipline enough to practice. Perhaps Jimmy Charles would be good at it. As the dry summer night settled around them, Abe tried to remember Jimmy Charles at center, making the long snap on punts, but the break was too great. Instead, he remembered Jimmy Charles turning a dive play into a forty-five-yard run and the winning touchdown in an important play-off game against someone in blue and white uniforms.

Abe ceremoniously honored the rites of autumn. He dragged his circus train combination of tandem disc and wheat drill across the dusty, dirty field, pledging his seeds of faith. Some farmers even questioned him directly this particular season. "Abe, aren't you afraid dragging this disc in front of the drill is going to dry out what little moisture you've got?"

He only answered, "I want to sow it deep so it will be there when the rains come." But they never did.

He ran his combine over fields of withered maize, looking for enough heads to merit making a few passages. Because of the light maize harvest and the methodical wheat sowing, he was days ahead of his fall schedule, but even that didn't bring him pleasure.

He stood along the sideline and faithfully watched the Whippets win game after game, games in which his own son was a starter; but even that didn't give him pleasure, at least, not like it should have. Change had come too abruptly for him. For years, he had anticipated the future and had watched it unfold; but now the reality was as hazy and dusty as the upper atmosphere during this drought. Things had gone awry. The whole world was transient.

He had moved through the season so methodically that the last regular season game came more as a matter of duty than celebration. The team was undefeated and playing well. This could be another state championship year. Jimmy Charles had adapted to his new role, and Abe had not heard any negative comments about his play at center. The long snaps had all been on target, and middle defensemen were blocked more often than not. Jimmy Charles still went through his pregame psychological preliminaries, but the postgame talk was casual and diversionary, never about the game, never about football.

As Abe took his place along the sidelines for that last home game, he noticed the dust in the sky had dimmed the stadium lights and his view of Mary Ruth sitting high in the stands. By the middle of the second quarter, the suspense had ended. Wheatheart was well in control, but Coach Rose continued to play masterful chess. This was, after all, his last game in this stadium. After thirty-one seasons, this was his final game, and the last thing he wanted to do was shock the fans with something new or different.

Of course, after the game there would be a huge celebration commemorating his career; but there would be no celebration, no levity, until the duty was done here first.

Through the dust, Abe watched the game as if it were miles away, something artificial, from a different and eerie world, almost. He had trouble concentrating. He did watch Jimmy Charles enough to know that he was getting the job done, but mostly Abe watched the backs. Michael Garland, who was now the left halfback, was having a good night. On the sweep around the end, he hip-faked to the outside, cut against the defensive flow, and found a large hole for a twelve-yard gain. As he was being dragged down, Abe casually checked the middle of the line, saw a big pile of human forms lying on the ground, and silently acknowledged Jimmy Charles' efficiency.

Abe's eyes then flirted around the perimeter of the play until he realized that movement was suspended. The pile of human forms in the middle was still there, and all the other bodies had stopped action to assess the delay. In the distance created by the dust, Abe couldn't distinguish as much as he would have liked, but he saw one player motion for help from the Wheatheart bench. Rambo rushed out quickly; Rose went slower but with a kind of purpose which always gave the home crowd confidence; and Doc Heimer ambled out to see if the incident deserved his attention.

Abe inventoried the standing players to ascertain the victim, and realized that it was Jimmy Charles. His mind flashed back to his own playing days when he had broken his arm on that very field, almost that same spot. He flinched when he remembered the pain, and he hoped for Jimmy Charles' sake that it wasn't a broken bone.

He glanced in the stands and saw Mary Ruth's face drawn tightly in either real or pretended fear that every mother shows when a player is on the ground. For her peace of mind, he decided that he would go out himself. That should help her relax her face. So he crawled under the cable and started a deliberate journey to the cluster of people in the middle of the field. This was the first time he had been on the field under the lights since he had finished here twenty-three years ago, and it felt strange—the grass, the huddled players, the eerie lights, the crowd behind instead of in front of him.

He gently nudged his way past the standing players who had circled the activity. He worked his way to a safe position which would allow him perspective but give the coach room to administer first aid. Jimmy Charles lay face up; his helmet had been removed, the chin strap cut away; his teeth guard lay away from the body as if it had been slung; his eyes were closed and Doc Heimer was viciously massaging his chest. All others stood nearby, lending only support of presence. Abe looked at the motionless body, and he looked at the face. As he looked a trickle of blood came out one ear, ran down the side of the cheek, stained the green grass red, then mingled into the soil of like color. But only Abe saw it. Abe knew then that he was looking at something he had never seen before, something that he shouldn't be looking at. This was too sacred to be stared at; so he turned away. Doc Heimer paused in his chest rubbing, bent his ear over the heart, listened intently, and then angrily declared to no one and to the whole world, "Well, this boy is dead!"

Traffic started early the next morning. Some came out of personal loss and sympathy. They wanted to help Abe and Mary Ruth cry, to show them that it was appropriate to cry. Some came out of duty. Some came out of curiosity. The caring ones stood around silently and stayed as if they had no better place to be. The dutybound ones politely and quickly announced their sympathy and left. The curiosity seekers stood on the periphery and chatted with each other about dust and drought. But all brought food.

Since Abe and Mary Ruth knew the community code, they had prepared themselves before the real parade began. They had spent time alone, and together. They really hadn't said that much. There wasn't much either could say. They couldn't even straighten their thinking yet; and feelings, those deep feelings, just couldn't be put into words. But through a mysterious process, like a young plant sucking moisture out of parched soil, they drew strength from being together, not necessarily from each other, because neither felt all that strong, but from the togetherness. In a bizarre kind of way, the events of the night before had drawn them closer than they had ever been before; but at the same time, those events had separated them. They weren't the same, not the two of them together. One of the things, perhaps the most important thing which had welded them together in marriage, had disappeared, and there was an awful gap.

Oh, it wasn't as if their relationship was about to break like an old piece of metal when the molecules get tired and quit. They still had things to hold them together, important things. They had the farm, and they had Wheatheart. But there still was an awful gap.

Doc Heimer came. He was one of the first. He was sorry, but he still insisted on assuring Abe and Mary Ruth that he had done all he could. He could have saved his speech. They knew that. Without discussing it with each other, they both somehow understood that no one could have done anything.

Brother Bob came. He knew the right words to say, and he said them; but it seemed to Abe almost as if the preacher had practiced his condolence, and would have been disappointed if he hadn't had the chance to use it occasionally. He took care of all the related business with a certain professional eagerness and tidiness which made Abe uneasy. There were occasions when efficiency was a waste of time, and this seemed to be one of them.

Mr. Benalli came and looked as if he intended to stay for a while, but tears kept coming into his eyes. He walked off by himself on a little private tour of the farm. When he came back, he had written some words on a scrap of paper. He handed it to Abe and left. Abe opened the note and managed to read aloud the first line, "Good night, sweet prince," before the tears covered his vision. Mary Ruth took the note as if she knew the rest of it, and put it away for a future time.

The football players came, some from sympathy, some from duty, and some from curiosity.

Finally, Coach Rose came. By then, Abe was receiving visitors at the barn. The house had closed him in. There were too many noises and too many distractions; and all that food seemed a vulgar token for filling a hunger which couldn't be satisfied.

Coach first stopped in the house to see Mary Ruth, then came to the barnyard where Abe seemed to be assessing the weight of the butcher calf. Without a word, the two men shook hands, as if by duty; but as they stood there too long to be comfortable, the coach reached his arm out and pulled Abe close and hugged him. In the wildest of the remembering, Abe had never imagined a situation where he would be embraced by Coach Rose. Something in him wanted to protest, but something deeper cherished the moment.

After the embrace, both men stood with their hands in their pockets and practiced punting the small pebbles around them. For the first time all morning, Abe wanted to talk, and he remembered how he had never been able to talk to the coach comfortably, man to man. But this was a new day.

Coach Rose managed to get the tears out of his throat first. "He was a good boy, Abe."

"Thanks, Coach."

"In all my years, I have never been close to one like I was to him. You love them all, like your sons, but Jimmy Charles was special."

Abe remembered that Jimmy Charles was an offensive center, but that didn't matter just now. "He always thought a lot of you." He was beginning to hate himself for this conversation. The coach was trying to help him, and he was acting like a sophomore player.

"Why, Abe?" Coach asked a rhetorical question.

"I've been working on that myself, Coach."

"Last summer, I intended to quit, Abe, to leave it completely; but I talked myself into one more season. This one last season. Thirty-one years without much more than a broken bone now and then, and in the last game . . . " His voice trailed away. "You just take so many chances, Abe, and it's bound to catch up with you."

For some reason, Abe took that moment to think about sowing wheat behind a tandem disc.

The coach continued, "Abe, what makes a man think he's always going to be on top? I should have known better. I have seen a lot of men fall and fall fast. We just take so much for granted. For more than thirty years I have had more than I deserved; but I would give it all up, every win and every trophy, to get your son back."

"I know, Coach," Abe replied, and he did know, or he was beginning to.

"Something in this world is permanent, Abe. I know there is. There has to be, but I don't know what it is. It isn't relationships. They come and they go, and I don't guess its life either. He was so alive one minute and only memory the next. What is there that's permanent?"

The idea haunted Abe, throughout the conversation and through-out the week. All that had been important had turned artificial. And the present moments seemed real, but it was all too shallow. None of it could root down to moisture and spring into any kind of promise of life. The duties such as picking the casket, the pallbear-ers, and the plot were once-in-a-lifetime activities which became just part of another day. The funeral service was another event, featuring Brother Bob in the pulpit; not bad but not unlike a thousand others, all running together; the journey to the cemetery in an artificial car with a strange operator, driving past fields which should have been green with young wheat plants but weren't, and past granaries which should have been filled with fresh-cut maize but weren't.

There, by the grave, Brother Bob read something from the Bible about sowing a grain of wheat and letting it die so it could spring back to life, and Abe thought of putting those poor seeds into those deep furrows chiseled by that tandem disc. And with that, the casket was lowered out of sight and reality.

That following Friday morning, Abe made two decisions from the stoop of the Culligan Soft Water place. He had already sent the telegram, as he and Mary Ruth had agreed and Wheatheart expect-ed. He had already filled his role, and had decided to have coffee and conversation at the Dew Drop Inn. Wheatheart was still Wheat-heart, and life was still life.

As he stood there in the November sun and surveyed the town even further, he went beyond the storefronts along Main Street, past the high school, even past the football field, and beyond all the physical memories; and he measured in his mind and in his heart what it meant to be a native, to belong to Wheatheart, to be a part of the heartbeat and the legend.

For a long time, maybe all his life, he had known what he received from that town. Now he should account for what he had given. Oh yes, he had given a son, but even more. He had given Wheatheart his devotion and loyalty. Obediently, he had lived by the code and practiced the rituals.

Even now, as he prepared to travel the block and a half to the Dew Drop Inn for morning coffee, that too would be by the code. Never mind the warmth of the sun, or the impulse for a little exercise. He would drive his pickup because Wheatheart farmers always drove their pickups any time they had to go farther than twenty yards. He smiled as he remembered the rule, and wondered how that silly practice ever got started. "We in Wheatheart have a rule for everything," he told himself; and he wanted to smile again. But he didn't. For suddenly, he remembered how lonely he was—lonely standing in the middle of Main Street on a Friday morning before an important football game.

He thought about that for a moment, thrust his thumbs in his overall bib, turned, and started walking defiantly down Main Street.